To:

MW01616756

Happy reading!

Suite Lies and Alibis

A Harmony Landing Mystery

Kristy T Dixon

Kristy J Dixon

For Vondelyn Smith

Chapter 1

I stared at the woman in front of me. Her expression was flat. No smile or even the smallest bit of humor showed on her face. She couldn't be serious.

She pushed her black hair behind her ear and peered at me over her reading glasses.

"Excuse me? I don't quite understand," I said. "If I buy the hotel, I have to promise to let the previous owner's nephew live and work there?"

"Yes," the realtor said, shuffling the papers on her desk. "It's not forever. You only have to agree to keep him on for ten years."

I bit my lip. "Ten years is a long time." Owning this hotel was my dream, and it was finally for sale. But ten years?

"That might be the reason no one has purchased the property. It's not as strange as you might think. Most people who acquire properties like this keep the employees who already work there. This just puts it in writing."

"Yes, but to have to keep him on makes me nervous." I couldn't hide the growing concern from my tone. "And to have him live there as well? It seems complicated. What if he's a horrible worker?"

"He does all the maintenance on the grounds and fixes anything that goes wrong inside. He's very handy, according to his aunt."

"Is he old?"

"Thirty-five, maybe?"

I slumped back in my chair across from the woman's desk and thought. It might not be terrible. But what if the guy was disagreeable? Or worse, a criminal? I didn't want to keep someone on who might cause problems, especially if he lived there.

"Forgive me for not being more attentive," the woman said. "I get inquiries about this property all the time, and no one buys it. It hardly seems worth my time."

"I've always wanted to own that hotel," I admitted.

"Is there a reason?"

"My name is Harmony Landing."

The woman looked over the rim of her black glasses. "Yes, the hotel is called Harmony Landing."

A small smile crossed my lips. "No, that's my name. I was named after the hotel. My parents met there when they were doing seasonal work one summer, and my dad's last name is Landing. They thought it was hilarious, so they named me after the place."

The woman raised her brow. "Interesting. I've never known anyone with the last name Landing. So, you want to buy the place your parents named you after?"

"Yep. Landing isn't a common name. There are only about four thousand people with the name, so I always know I'm related if I meet someone with the same name."

"How fun," she said with no expression. Great. I was spouting off boring facts. "There is something else you might want to consider before you purchase it."

"Something worse than it coming with a nephew?"

"Possibly. Someone died there a few years back, and it's become a big legend in the town."

"Things like that don't bother me. The nephew is my worry."

"Have you ever even seen the hotel?"

"Only in pictures," I admitted.

"Don't you want to see it in person?"

"Yes. I was going to have the cab take me over before I came here, but I didn't want someone else beating me to it, and it's a long drive."

The woman laughed. "It's been for sale for over a year."

"Really?" I frowned. "I look it up every so often. I've never seen it listed until two days ago."

"You flew here to buy a hotel you've never seen?"

I pushed a strand of reddish-brown hair behind my ear. "Yes. Isn't it your job to sell the property? I feel like you're trying to get me to pass."

"I would love it if you bought it. I just don't want to waste my time if you aren't serious."

"I'm serious. I've been saving my entire adult life for this." It was weird, but I'd dreamed of owning the hotel from the moment I heard the story of my name twenty-five years ago.

"How far is it from here?"

"About a thirty-minute drive. Are you pre-approved for a loan?"

"I don't need a loan. I can pay cash."

Her eyes went wide. "That's some nice saving you've done. Well, if it's a cash sale, I would love to work with you."

I should have worn better clothing. She probably thought I was broke. I looked down at my jeans and green T-shirt and frowned. They didn't look that bad.

I'd saved a lot over the years, but I'd also inherited a large sum when I turned eighteen. I hadn't touched any of it, just waiting for this.

"Great," I said, smiling. "Let's get started."

I stood in front of the Harmony Landing Hotel and smiled. The five-story hotel looked like a dream. I knew I was looking at it through rose-colored glasses, but I didn't care. It wasn't a new building, but someone had cared for it—or it looked like it from the outside.

The coral stucco was slightly weathered, but not enough to draw attention unless a person was looking. A few of the rooms had balconies, framed by wrought-iron railings, and the red roof glistened in the sun. The beach was a block away, so the upper floors would have a nice view of the ocean.

I'd stayed in the same city as the relator's office until everything was final, but I'd been itching to get here. As soon as I signed the last paper, I called an Uber and came as fast as I could.

I took a deep breath, smelling the salty ocean air. At least, I assumed that was what I was smelling. I'd never been near the ocean before.

Palm trees lined the front of the hotel, and I resisted the urge to touch one. Who knew trees could look like that? I could already tell I would love the West Coast.

I entered through the sliding glass doors and nodded at the young man loading luggage onto a cart. Knowing he was my employee made me want to giggle.

A group of teens in swimming suits ran past me, and I jumped out of the way to avoid being trampled.

I'd dressed carefully today to give off a good impression. A pressed blouse, black slacks, and just enough make-up to look polished, but not overdone. I didn't obsess over my looks, but I knew what I saw in the mirror. Long auburn hair and hazel eyes that don't ever settle on an exact color.

I walked through the lobby and up to the front desk and beamed at a woman behind the counter. She had the brightest red hair I'd ever seen—and lipstick to match. She looked about fifty, but I've never been good at guessing ages.

"Hello, Marla," I said, reading her nametag.

"Hi, darlin'. What can I do for ya?" she said in a heavy southern accent.

"I'm Harmony Landing."

She raised her brow.

"I'm the new owner of the hotel."

"Oh!" Marla said, coming out from behind the desk. "I'm thrilled to meet ya!" She gave me a hug, and I felt the warmth of her welcome seep into me; I was going to like Marla. "I was expecting someone a little bit older."

I only smiled. I was thirty-one, which felt old enough to me.

"What's your name, hon?" she asked.

"Harmony Landing. I know. It's weird, and I'm going to confuse everyone. My parents met at this hotel."

"How lovely!" she said. "You are going to get some funny looks every time you introduce yourself to anyone around here. Did you know Cathy?"

"Who?"

"The previous owner?"

"No, I never met her."

"She wanted me to take you straight to Chase when you got here."

"And that's her nephew, right?"

"Yes, a darlin' man. Most people don't agree with me on that, but give him a chance. He's the most helpful person here. I swear we'd all fall apart without him. He changes lightbulbs, mows the grass, fixes broken appliances. There isn't anything that man can't do, except maybe carry on a normal conversation."

"Why do I need to meet him first?" I asked. I still wasn't happy about having to agree to keep the man on. The staff were all welcome to stay, but it would be nice to be able to let someone go if I needed to.

"He's the one to go to if you need anything. Come on, I'll run ya over to his room."

I followed Marla down a tan hallway. We weaved around hotel guests, most dressed for the beach. Marla wore a bright purple knee-length dress and pink heels. It was an interesting choice of clothing, but it suited her.

"Is this your first time in Crystal Rock?" she asked.

"Yes."

"How do you like it so far?"

"I just got in, but it's beautiful."

We stopped at the last room in the back corner, and Marla pounded on the door. "Open up, Chase!" she called. "I brought the new boss lady to meet ya."

The door opened a crack, and a man with a long brown beard poked his head out. He looked at me, and his eyes narrowed. His mustache covered his lips, and his beard appeared uneven. The length of his hair almost matched his beard.

"She's the new owner?" he asked. The man rolled his eyes and slammed the door.

"He seems friendly," I said as I swallowed my rising doubts.

Marla banged on the door again. "Open the door right this minute, Chase Jensen!"

He opened it again. "Come on, Marla. What do you want with me?"

"Meet Harmony. You know more about this place than anyone, and she's going to need your guidance."

"Her name's Harmony? She doesn't look old enough to run this place."

"I'm thirty-one," I said. "I have a degree in business. I'm not completely incompetent."

He opened the door. "Whatever, come in."

I entered, and it looked like any other hotel room I'd been in. There was a double bed and a nightstand with a lamp. Across from the bed was a chest of drawers and a TV mounted to the wall. A sofa sat against the far wall under the window. Tucked away in a corner, there was a compact kitchen area with an oven, a refrigerator, and a microwave. Although dated, it all seemed clean and organized.

"Where did Marla go?" I asked when he shut the door.

"To the front desk, I assume."

I nodded. "So, you're Chase Jensen?"

"Yep."

I held out my hand. "I'm Harmony Landing."

He blinked as he shook my hand but didn't speak.

"Marla said you have things to tell me?"

He rubbed the back of his neck. "Not really. If you need anything, you can text me and I'll fix it or whatever. I do all the maintenance."

I wondered about his appearance. The beard and hair were a bit wild, but his clothing was neat, and his hair wasn't greasy or anything.

"Do you drive?" I asked.

"You mean, can I drive?"

"Like, if I need to go somewhere, can you drive me?"

He tilted his head. "I suppose. Don't you know how to drive?"

"I know how... but it turns out your license gets suspended if you get too many tickets."

"I see."

I tried to figure out why Chase had the beard and hair he did. I could tell he would be attractive without them—if his eyes were any indication. He had nice brown eyes, too. Even if he simply trimmed the beard so it was even, it might help.

"So, if I buy a car, can you add chauffeur to your list of duties?"

His eyes narrowed. "I suppose, but I'm not wearing a stupid hat."

"Wonderful. Is there anything else I need to know?"

He shrugged. "This is the kind of thing you have to learn as you go."

"Why do you want to stay here if your aunt left?"

"I don't follow my aunt. I've worked here forever. It's a good job."

"Well, if there's nothing else, I should find my cottage." There was supposedly a small cottage behind the hotel where the former owner had lived. It would keep me close but separated at the same time.

"I can walk you there," he said, opening the door and walking out. He didn't hold it for me, but he didn't slam it in my face. That had to be progress.

I followed him as we went back down the hallway and out the front doors. The air was humid, and I wondered what it was doing to my hair. I could feel it poking out at odd angles. We walked around the hotel, past a pool, through a parking lot, and down a curvy sidewalk that went to a small cottage with a green door and shutters.

I smiled. More palm trees.

"It's so cute!" I exclaimed. The grass around the cottage was neatly cut, and big orange flowers I didn't recognize grew near the door.

Chase didn't say anything.

The roof looked new, and the paint was fresh.

I pulled the key from my pocket.

"I do maintenance on the cottage as well as the hotel and take care of the yard."

"Is there a lot of maintenance?"

"The hotel is fifty years old. A lot of things need to be replaced, but my aunt liked to have me repair things, not fix the real problem. I'm busy most of the day just with upkeep."

I nodded. I'd expected that. I would keep records of the worst problems and fix them as I could.

A Golden Retriever came running around the corner of the house, barking. His tail was wagging, so I wasn't too worried.

"Samson!" Chase said, dropping to his knees. The dog bounded over to him and began licking his face. "What are you still doing here?" he asked, rubbing the dog behind the ears. He looked at me. "My Aunt Cathy said she was taking him. She's already halfway across the country. I can't believe she would forget him. Let me give her a call."

Chase sat on the ground, fussing over Samson, and pulled out his phone.

The dog sat on Chase's lap, sticking his head in Chase's face. I wasn't sure how to feel about Chase, but the dog certainly liked him.

"Hey, Aunt Cathy," he said into his phone. "You forgot Samson." He listened for a minute, and then his brows creased. "No, you never said that. Nope. Positive. I can't take care of him, he can't stay in the hotel. Well, what do you want me to do? You have to send for him... no. No." He growled and put his phone down.

"She forgot her dog?" That seemed impossible to me. How could someone forget a pet?

"She claims I agreed to keep him. She probably thinks we had that conversation, but it must have been in her head."

"Did he stay in the cottage?" I looked from the cottage to Samson.

"Yes, but I took care of him. He's probably starving. I didn't feed him today because I thought he was gone."

"He can stay with me."

"That won't go well. Samson's a good dog, but he doesn't warm up to people quickly."

I went closer and held up my hand. "Come here, Samson."

Samson sniffed me, and I ran my hand over his head. He jumped off Chase's lap and wagged his tail as I continued to pet him.

"I think he likes me."

Chase just frowned.

Chapter 2

By noon the next day, I'd walked all over the hotel and gone into almost every room that didn't have people staying in it. The rooms were all the same, except some had one bed and some had two. None were any better than the others unless you took the view into account. From the third floor up, I could see the ocean. It seemed to go on forever, and I couldn't wait to go explore the beach.

Now that I'd been walking around and assessing so much—and the stars were no longer in my eyes—I saw some of the problems Chase had mentioned. Things looked neat, but there were places where the floor sagged, and the bathrooms all looked like they needed new floors and fixtures. I didn't know how to describe the smell of old, but this place had it. I hoped it wasn't mold.

I opened a door, ready to see the same room I'd already seen several times, but this one had heavier curtains, which made it darker.

A noise came from the right.

I stilled. It was coming from the bathroom.

Hesitating, I took a deep breath, but walked carefully over. Then, I pulled open the door before I could convince myself otherwise.

A woman spun around and screamed.

My body tensed, and I took a step back, letting out a small shriek.

"What are you doing here?" she asked, wielding a toilet scrubber like a sword.

"I own this place. What are you doing?" I asked.

"I'm sorry," she said and lowered her weapon. "I'm with housekeeping." She was probably around my age. Her black hair was pulled back in a tight ponytail, and she wore jeans and a button-up shirt. The only thing that would make a person think she was part of the staff was a badge around her neck. We must not have a dress code for employees.

"Shouldn't you have a cart?" I asked.

She frowned. "Yes, I'm sorry. Just seems like a waste to clean this room, so I didn't want to bring all my stuff over here."

"Why wouldn't you clean this room?"

She shrugged. "Because we don't rent this one out."

"Never?"

She shook her head. "Well, occasionally, but not often."

"Ohhh," I said, looking around with greater interest. "Is this the *haunted* room?" I'd heard a few people mention a haunted room.

I expected her to laugh, but she nodded instead. "The less time I spend here, the better. I guess we do rent it out every once in a while. There are people who want to sleep in a haunted room. Usually around Halloween."

"I'm Harmony," I said. "What's your name?"

"Samantha Diaz."

"Nice to meet you. Can you tell me why people think the room is haunted?" I asked.

"Someone was killed here once. Now people hear odd things when they come in here."

"Like what?" I didn't believe in ghosts, so I wasn't worried.

"Sometimes people hear a clock ticking, but there isn't that type of clock anywhere in the hotel. Things will crash around. Sometimes I have to take out garbage that shouldn't be here, or the bed will be messy. It smells funny inside sometimes, like someone's been microwaving cheap burritos. The toilet should always be clean and unused, but occasionally it's not."

My lip twitched, almost a smile. "I doubt a ghost would use the bathroom and eat burritos."

"Perhaps not, but someone uses it, even when no one should've been in here."

"Who was killed here?"

"I don't know who she was. It was years before I started working here."

So, it was a woman. "Did they catch the killer?"

"No. There wasn't enough evidence. Everyone knows who did it, though."

"Oh?"

She glanced around like someone might be listening, then leaned forward and whispered, "It was Chase Jensen."

My eyes narrowed. "And he still lives here?"

"He claimed it wasn't him, but everyone knows it was. He was never convicted."

"Have you ever talked to him?"

"Once. Scared me to death. I get a chill every time I see him. They say he used to be a handsome man with a lot going for him. Now nobody wants to deal with him. He hasn't cut his hair or beard since it happened."

I frowned. "If there wasn't enough evidence, we probably shouldn't decide he's guilty."

She shrugged. "Maybe not. Like I said. I wasn't here when it happened. I only know what everyone says."

I looked around the room. "If it scares you to clean the room, you don't have to do it. I don't believe in ghosts, so I'll do it."

"Thanks," she said. "I really hate it in here. It's not so bad when someone else is with me, but man, it gives me shivers." As if on cue, she shuddered.

"What's your job title?" I asked. I needed to make sure I had all the correct terminology down, so I didn't offend anyone.

"Housekeeper. I also translate all the hotel's flyers and emails into Spanish. I do that after hours when I get home."

"Nice. I hope we pay you for that?"

"Yes. Cathy didn't like to spend money on updating the hotel, but she paid well."

I let Samantha go back to cleaning the next room, and I found the cleaning supplies and grabbed a duster. I went into the room and began dusting all the surfaces.

Samantha must've really been neglecting the room. Clumps of dust fell everywhere I went.

I pulled open the curtains and let in some natural light. That made the room a lot more welcoming. I began humming. I was so excited to know this place was mine.

After a few minutes, I heard a ticking clock. It was normally something I wouldn't notice, but since Samantha had mentioned the sound, I paused and looked around. I couldn't tell where the sound was coming from, so I shrugged. There had to be a reasonable explanation.

Once the room was clean, I went and found Marla at the front desk. Today, she wore a red dress with blue heels. She definitely had her own style.

"Hi, Marla. How are you today?"

"Great, hon. Have you explored the place?"

"Yep. Samantha was telling me we don't rent out the *haunted* room. Is there a reason to keep it around? I mean, we could tear it down and make it into something else so it wouldn't bother people."

"People would still avoid the area. Except for the few crazies who want to stay there."

"How often does that happen?"

"Not a lot."

"How long have you worked here?" I asked.

"Only about five months."

"Are you from the area?" I wanted to ask more about Chase and the murder, and Marla took me as the type who liked to talk.

"No. I'm originally from Georgia, and most recently, Kansas."

"What brought you here?" It would serve me well to get to know my employees, even if I wanted more information on the murder at the same time.

"I like change. I had a high-stress job, and it all just became too much. Now I work here and spend my evenings reading on the beach. It's the perfect place for me. It's like living in a postcard."

"What's that small area over there?" I asked, pointing to a small room with a gate that kept people out. It was off to the side of the front doors. It reminded me of a vacant store in a mall.

"That used to be the gift shop," Marla said. "It didn't do well, apparently. Cathy shut it down about a year ago, so I never saw it in action."

My eyes lit up. "We should turn it into a small bakery."

"There's no baking equipment here."

"I could make it in my cottage, and we could sell it here."

Marla tapped a finger on her chin in thought. "That might not be a bad idea. The hotel doesn't have any breakfast, so maybe you could do breakfast pastries? I bet those would sell. People have to go out to a restaurant or use the kitchens for every meal when they stay here."

My mind raced through ideas as I walked up and down the hallway. I already had a food handler's permit. It wouldn't be a hard thing to do. I could start with just breakfast muffins and slowly work up from there. I would have to find someone to turn the area into a cute little breakfast nook. There was probably space to put in a display case to show off the pastries and maybe three or four small round tables.

I hurried off to my cottage so I could google some things.

When I got there, Chase and Samson were playing outside. The dog saw me and ran over, and I rubbed his head.

"Hello, sweetheart," I said. He'd stayed in the cottage with me last night and hadn't given me any trouble. He'd followed me around, wagging his tail and watching everything I did.

"Hi, Chase. How's it going?"

He just grunted.

"I'm thinking of turning the old gift shop into a small area to buy breakfast foods. Is that something you can do, or should I hire someone?"

His blank expression didn't change. "I can do it."

"Great. I'm going to make a few plans, then I'll give them to you."

"You'll need a permit."

"I'll get one."

Chase nodded but didn't leave. He sat in the grass, looking at me. Nothing in his face gave me any sign of what he was thinking.

I wouldn't let him unnerve me, so I stared back. It didn't take long for me to feel ridiculous. He didn't look phased, and I was trying not to twitch.

"I cleaned the haunted room today," I said.

He blinked hard, and I held in a victorious grin.

I patted Samson's head. "I don't think it's actually haunted. Samantha seems to think it is, but I think it's her imagination."

"Of course it's not haunted," he muttered. He plucked some blades of grass and threw them. "All the staff scare each other. When a new person starts, they freak them out, so no one wants to go inside."

"I'm going to clean the room since it bothers people. I did hear a clock ticking while I was in there."

"You did?"

"Yeah. I couldn't tell where it was coming from."

"And that didn't scare you?" Chase sounded genuinely interested.

I laughed. "It was a clock. If it were a ghost, I seriously doubt there would be a ticking."

"I've never heard anything in there."

"It only lasted a few seconds. I wouldn't have noticed if someone hadn't told me."

He stood up and walked away without saying goodbye. He was an interesting character.

I went inside and grabbed my laptop. Samson was right behind me. I had planned on googling small bakeries, but I googled Chase Jensen and the Harmony Landing Hotel in its place. Nothing came up, so I googled 'a murder at Harmony Landing Hotel.'

A story popped up, and I began reading. There wasn't much to it. A woman who had lived here had died, and poison had been found in her coffee. She was only twenty-nine. It said there were no suspects except the woman's boyfriend, who she had fought with earlier, but there was no evidence.

I rubbed my finger back and forth across my lip as I thought. Chase must have been the boyfriend. It looked like it had happened a little over five years ago. I gave Samson a treat and went back to the hotel to talk to Marla.

She was sitting at the front desk, staring at the computer.

"Sorry to keep bothering you, Marla," I said.

"You're no bother, hun," she said. "What do you need?"

"How many people actually live at the hotel?"

"Well, there's Chase, of course, then Sherman Bradley, and Harvey Vaughn. Just the three."

"Is it normal for people to live in a hotel?"

"It's not common, but it happens."

"The woman who died here? She lived here?"

"That's what I heard."

"And she dated Chase?"

Marla frowned. "You aren't listening to gossip now, are you? That man wouldn't hurt a fly. Well, maybe a fly, but he's no killer."

"But they dated?" I pressed.

"I wasn't around, so I can't say for sure. You could ask the sheriff. He might not want to answer, though. He and Chase go way back, like cornbread and butter."

"You mean they're friends?"

"Yep. They're tighter than bark on a tree. The sheriff is the only person Chase talks to willingly."

"It just makes me nervous thinking someone at the hotel could be a murderer. Gossip usually comes from some truth."

"All I've heard is the gossip, and there's one thing I know about gossip. It's usually only twenty-five percent true."

Chapter 3

The next day, I knocked on Chase's door. I'd expected to spend the first week in the hotel getting familiar with it, but all I could think about was the haunted room and the mysterious Chase Jensen. I couldn't ask him anything directly, because that would be insensitive, especially if he'd been dating the woman.

The door opened, and he peeked out. "What?"

"I know I asked if you would drive me around, but I don't have a way to go buy a car. I know the town is fairly small, so I'm guessing I can't get a car here?"

"Have you even looked around the town?" he asked. "We're a tourist place. You can find great food, lodging, and water activities. What you won't find is a car dealership."

"I've only driven through on my way to the hotel. I haven't seen anything really."

His eyes narrowed. "You bought a hotel in a place you don't know and haven't researched?"

I shrugged. "I've always wanted to own this hotel. I never thought much about the town."

"Hmm."

I wanted to ask what he was thinking, but didn't. He probably thought I was irresponsible. I guess I was sometimes. I was often less detail-oriented than I should have been. After all these years, I hadn't researched the town. All I'd cared about was the name and that it was in a place with nice weather.

"And you wanted this hotel because...?"

"It has my name."

"Right. Harmony was it?"

I tried not to roll my eyes. "Yes. Harmony Landing. My parents met here thirty-four years ago."

"I have a truck. If you don't mind riding in it, I don't mind using it if you don't want to buy a car right now."

"That would be great. I'll pay you extra for gas and wear on the truck. I don't have any groceries and have been living off of sandwiches. Could you take me to the store?"

"Please."

"Excuse me?"

"Will you *please* take me to the store? You missed that part."

I rolled my eyes. This coming from someone who had slammed the door in my face the first time we met? "Will you please take me to the store?"

"Yep. When?"

"Now?"

Chase sighed. "Let me get my shoes." He shut the door, and I stood in the hall waiting. I felt funny standing there as people passed.

I wondered if it was stupid of me to get into a car with someone people thought might be a murderer, but he didn't make me feel uncomfortable, and I trusted Marla. If Marla said there was nothing to the rumors, I believed her. I carried mace in my purse, just in case, but I was almost sure I wouldn't need it.

Chase came out and walked away without a word, so I followed him out to the parking lot. He climbed into a blue truck.

I paused and wondered if I should just get in. I didn't feel awkward often, but I was beginning to think that might change if I spent a lot of time around Chase.

I climbed in and buckled my seatbelt.

Chase pulled out of the hotel parking lot and onto the street. I stared out the window as the small town passed by. This street was almost completely full of restaurants, but we did pass another hotel. It was smaller than my hotel, and it looked older and more run-down. I knew that shouldn't make me feel good, but it did.

"It's neat to be close to the ocean," I said. Chase didn't speak. "Have you always lived here?"

"Yes."

"Do you like it?"

"It's fine."

He wasn't elaborating, so I stopped talking as we pulled into a parking lot. The store was only two blocks east and one block south of the hotel. I could walk here without a problem when I only needed a few things.

I jumped out of the car and waited. When Chase remained inside, I walked around to his side, and he rolled down the window.

"Aren't you coming in?" I asked.

"No."

"You're just going to sit in the car?"

"Yep."

I shrugged and went inside.

A crease settled between my brows as I entered. If this were the only grocery store in town, I would have to drive to the next town to shop. Especially if I planned on buying in bulk to reduce costs for the baked goods. This one only had seven aisles, and they were short. I walked through the entire store in two minutes. Everything was overpriced. I grabbed a few things and put them in the mini cart.

"Is that Chase Jensen in the parking lot?" I heard a woman say.

I turned. A woman about my age with a short, bleached ponytail was standing next to me. I couldn't tell if she was talking to me or herself, but she was looking out the window at Chase's truck.

"It is," I said, since I was the only other person in the store.

She jumped slightly and turned her eyes to me. "Do I know you?"

"I'm Harmony," I said, holding out my hand. "I just bought Harmony Landing Hotel."

She shook my hand and flashed her white teeth. "How nice! I wondered if anyone would ever buy that old place. Did Chase bring you? I don't see any other cars."

"Yes."

"I'm McKenzie Taylor. I own this store."

"It's nice to meet you." I let go of her hand.

"How did you get Chase to come here?"

"I asked him to drive me."

"And he did?"

I wanted to say, 'Obviously,' but I just nodded.

"Interesting. Chase hasn't come to the store in years."

"Oh?" I asked, hoping for any gossip I could get about Chase.

"I'm sure you heard about the murder at the hotel? After it happened, Chase stopped socializing and kept to the hotel. People blamed him for the death, so if he has to shop, I hear he goes to another town. It's really too bad. He had a lot going for him."

It might be easier to get information in this town than I thought. McKenzie seemed willing to lay this all out to a complete stranger.

"Do you know him well?" I asked.

"I did before he became a hermit. We both grew up here and went to school together. I probably knew him better than anyone. We were pretty good friends. Even dated a little. I should probably go out and say hello."

"Can I check out first?"

"Sure," she said, hurrying over to one of two registers. She scanned my things quickly, then rushed out the door.

I followed with my bags.

McKenzie knocked on the window of Chase's truck, and he stared at her—almost through her.

"Hey, Chase!" she said. "It's so good to see you out and about town!"

Left with no choice, Chase rolled down the window. "Hi, McKenzie. I don't have time to chat."

I put my stuff in the back of the truck and got in the passenger seat.

"There's always time to chat with old friends," she said. "You've been ignoring my texts and calls for years. You know, people are worried about you."

"I'm fine."

"Why don't you come in and we can catch up?"

"I don't think so."

"Why not?"

"There are so many reasons." Chase rolled up the window, and we drove off, leaving McKenzie gaping after us.

I sat quietly while Chase fumed. Since I didn't know the story and I barely knew him, I figured it was none of my business. Keeping my mouth shut wasn't easy, and it made me squirm in my seat. I wasn't sure why I wanted to know Chase's history so much.

Although it seemed Chase held no affection for McKenzie, she didn't appear scared of him in the slightest. Quite the opposite.

"I went to cosmetology school for a while," I said when we pulled into the hotel's lot. That was my limit for being quiet. "I didn't graduate or anything, but I can give a decent haircut."

Chase whipped the truck sharply into a space and turned off the truck, got out, and slammed the door.

I hurried out of my seat and ran to catch up to him as he stormed toward the building. "I wasn't saying I wanted to cut your hair," I said, trying to keep up with his long strides. "I didn't mean to offend you or anything."

"It's fine," Chase said, not looking at me. He entered the hotel and strode toward his room.

I followed. "Where do you eat?"

He stopped and turned to me. "What?"

"The hotel doesn't have food, so where do you eat?"

His jaw ticked. "I have a small kitchen in my room. It's not hard to microwave things."

"How about, as part of your pay for running me around, I'll bring you meals?"

He raised his brows. "Why?"

"If you're helping me so often, you should at least get a good meal. Cooking for two people is actually easier than cooking for one person, so it wouldn't be any extra work for me."

"Did you go to culinary school as well as cosmetology school?" Chase looked like he might be smiling slightly, but it was hard to tell behind the facial hair.

"Maybe for a few months."

"And you have a degree in business. How many schools did you go to?"

I pressed my lips together and crossed my arms. "A few. It's not easy to know what you want to do with your life when you're young. Sometimes it takes a few tries. So can I make you meals?"

"One a day," he said.

"Which meal would you prefer?"

He shrugged. "It doesn't matter."

"I'll bring dinner."

He nodded and left.

I watched him and wondered what was wrong with me. I'd always loved a mystery, and this guy was definitely that. I didn't take him as a murderer, but I could be wrong.

Either way, I was making it my goal to figure out what really happened in room 202—the *haunted* room.

"What are you up to?" Marla asked, coming up behind me.

I jumped and shook my head, trying to clear my thoughts. "Just thinking... Oh!" I said. "I left my groceries in Chase's truck."

"Chase took you to the store?" Marla smiled. "You might be just the thing this place needs. I'll help you get your groceries."

We went back out, grabbed my bags, and walked around the outside of the hotel. It was becoming a familiar path.

"Do you think the room at the hotel is haunted?" I asked as I unlocked my door.

Marla went into the cottage when I opened it. "Well, that's hard to say. I've never been in there. There has been more than one staff member come scurrying out claiming something happened, though."

"What about the rooms under and above the haunted room? Do people hear anything when they're in those rooms?"

"Well, I've never heard Harvey Vaughn complain in the upstairs room. He wouldn't, though, because he's our security guard. He would check it out himself. The room below it belongs to Sherman Bradley. He's lived here for about ten years. We put the people who live here one on top of the other, so they aren't dealing with tourists coming in at all times of the night."

"Ten years? I can't believe anyone would live in a hotel for that long. Especially one without a restaurant. The kitchens in these rooms are so small."

"He's a millionaire. He eats out every meal and rarely touches his kitchen. He never opens his curtains. Crazy, isn't it?"

"That is crazy. What's Sherman Bradley like? Would he talk to me?"

"He's an interesting man. He's easy enough to talk to. I don't have a really solid opinion of him. He does like to complain about everything." She laughed fondly. "If you let him, he'll tell you all his problems until you pass out from boredom."

"If he's a millionaire, why stay here? There are nicer hotels."

Marla shrugged. "I don't know. It's close to everything, and this hotel is better than the other two in the town. He's from here originally, so I guess he wants to stay in town."

"Aren't there apartments?"

"Yes. I really don't know why he does it. Housekeeping, maybe?"

"And Harvey?"

"He's a retired policeman. He's about sixty-five. I believe his rent is free since he does security here."

"I haven't met him."

"He was out of town until yesterday. He's a character. Probably my favorite of all the employees here. Has a magnifying glass and a black light, and when he gets bored, he goes around trying to find anything that might be wrong. The housekeepers hate it, because he finds spots that can't be seen without the black light and tells them they should scrub it."

I smiled. "That would be annoying."

"He's fun."

"Do you like mysteries?"

Marla grinned. "I love them, hon. I sometimes think I should have been a detective."

I put my bags on the small kitchen table. "Do you want to help me figure out the mystery of room 202?"

Marla's smile got bigger. "Do I ever. I've been dying to know the truth, but I get nervous about snooping. Since you own the place, that fixes that. And if we can figure it out, poor Chase gets to live a normal life."

"What do you mean?"

"Since everyone thinks he's guilty, he avoids people. From what I've been told, he was a funny, charming man before it happened. After, he grew that massive facial atrocity and cut himself off. It's hard to get a word out of him. A lot of people only started blaming him when they thought the room was haunted. They think the girl who died there isn't able to rest until justice is served."

I put the food away as I thought. "I wonder what he would look like if he shaved."

"Handsome for sure. I would go for him even with the beard if I were twenty or so years younger." She giggled. "I like a man with muscles, and he has those."

"So, where do we start?" I asked with a grin.

"Don't know. Asking Chase questions would probably be the best thing to do, but he's not going to go for that."

I leaned against the countertop and pursed my lips. "We have to figure out why the room is supposedly haunted. I bet there's something to it. Either someone did something to make it scary, or it's people's imaginations."

"How do we figure it out?"

My eyes lit up. "We could spend the night there."

Marla's perfect brow raised. "Spend the night? Why not start in the morning?"

"Wouldn't night be the time a place is more haunted?"

Marla shrugged. "I suppose so."

"Do you live close by?"

"Only a minute's walk."

"Do you need to tell someone you won't be home tonight?"

"Tonight? You sure don't waste time. I live alone, so it's not a problem."

Marla had to go back to the front desk, so I started planning dinner. I didn't want to disappoint Chase and make something awful, but I didn't want to make something so good that he expected something exceptional every day.

I grabbed the pack of pork chops I'd just gotten and realized I only had one pan, and it was a pot, not a frying pan. I didn't have much of anything. My parents were going to send all my things in a moving truck, but that wouldn't be here for three more days. I put the pork back and frowned. I grabbed the pot and decided on a stew.

One of the first things I'd learned to make in school was stew. My teacher said that if you could make a stew that wasn't bland, then you could make anything. I'd gotten pretty good. I began peeling potatoes, and then I cut carrots.

This was going to be the best stew Chase Jensen had ever tasted.

Chapter 4

It took me some time to find Chase after I finished making the stew. When I tracked him down, he was fixing a leaky sink.

"You're hard to find," I said. "I have your dinner."

He looked up from the sink. "Can you leave it in my room? I'll be done in a minute."

"Is it locked?"

"No."

"Alright." I went back to his place and left the stew on his small counter. It shocked me that anyone could live in such a small space. It would drive me crazy.

After dropping off the food, I played with Samson outside and fed him. He was too big to be kept in a cottage all the time, so I needed to figure out a way to give him more space so he could run around and get his energy out. He liked to play rough, and that made me nervous.

Whenever Samson saw Chase, they rolled around and played, but I preferred the more mellow parts of having a dog. I could picture the two of us going on pleasant walks by the ocean at sunset. Once I was more familiar with the town, we would do it.

Back at the hotel, I paced while waiting for Marla to get off. When she did, we went to room 202.

"It doesn't look haunted," Marla said after she flipped on the light.

My nose scrunched up. "Do all hotels smell so musty?" I asked. "I wonder if there's any way to get rid of the smell."

Marla crossed her arms. "We could try air fresheners. We aren't really gonna sleep here, are we?"

I looked at Marla's outfit. There was no way she could sleep comfortably in it. It was a green dress that fell to her knees. I was wearing jeans, so that wouldn't be comfortable either.

"No, but we'll stay in here for a while and see if anything happens." I sat on the bed and sighed. "Are all the beds here this hard? It feels awful. I'm going to have to check, because that's no way to run a hotel."

"We've had complaints," Marla said, sitting on the other bed. "We're a three-star hotel. The only thing that makes that okay is that the other hotels in town are two stars."

She glanced around. "So, now what? We just sit here and hope something happens?"

I shrugged. "I'm not sure."

The ticking sound began, slow and mechanical, just like before.

I froze and looked at Marla. "Do you hear that?" I asked.

She nodded. "It sounds like it's coming from the floor."

I dropped to the floor and put my ear against the flat blue carpet. The musty smell hit me, and I cringed.

With my ear pressed to the ground, I crawled slowly, following the sound until it felt like it was right below me.

It stopped.

A moment later, the sound came from above. I stared up at the ceiling.

I stood and looked up. "How did it move? I was about ready to tear up the floor to see if there was a clock in there." I jumped on one of the orangish bedspreads to get closer to the sound. As soon as I got up, it stopped, and started again in the wall.

"This is just weird," Marla said, going to the wall and putting her ear to it. "What do you suppose it is?"

"Not a ghost. A ghost doesn't tick."

"Look," Marla said, pointing at the wall.

The picture above the bed swayed sluggishly from side to side.

Since I was already on the bed, I went over and grabbed the picture. I pulled it back to see what was behind it, but

I pulled too hard and it came off the wall. The weight of it surprised me, and I dropped it on the floor.

I cringed. "Wow, that was loud. Do you think anyone heard that?"

"Probably," Marla said, picking up the painting. "The corner of the frame is broken."

I ran my hand over the wall. "Nothing seems weird. I might have to tear the entire room apart to get to the bottom of this."

"Aren't you even a little scared?" Marla asked, her hands twisting around one another.

"Not exactly scared. Maybe a little nervous," I said. "There has to be some type of explanation. We just have to figure out what."

"Well, I sure have the shivers. Look up at the light cover."

I glanced up, and it looked like bugs were crawling all over inside.

"I bet they aren't real," I said, jumping on the bed to try to see inside. "Someone is up to something."

I jumped again, and when I landed, the bed made a loud crunching noise and collapsed. I fell onto the mattress and looked at Marla.

"Someone heard that for sure," Marla said.

We both started laughing.

"It's a good thing I own the place, and that we don't use this room." I climbed off the bed, and my mouth turned down. "I hope all the beds aren't that flimsy."

"Two have broken since I've worked here."

I sighed. "I hope this place doesn't turn into a money pit."

"Chase was always telling his aunt they needed to replace things instead of trying to fix them cheaply."

So I'd heard.

I looked back at the light and squealed. Little spiders were crawling all over the light and the ceiling. It looked like they were pouring out of a crack where the light was mounted. I wasn't scared of make-believe ghosts, but spiders were a different thing.

"Goodness gracious!" Marla said, stepping as far away from the light as she could get. She pressed herself against the wall and put a hand to her heart.

I moved near her. "I don't do spiders."

"Me neither."

The door burst open, and Chase came running in. He looked from the broken bed to the painting, to the two of us standing against the wall.

"What's going on in here?" he demanded.

I pointed at the ceiling, and he looked up. His eyes narrowed—and he might have frowned. I wished he would shave so I could read him better.

"Please tell me you weren't throwing things at the spiders?" he said, looking at the painting.

"No," I said, not taking my eyes off the spiders.

"What are you two doing in here?"

"We were trying to figure out why people think this place is haunted," I said.

"By busting things up? I'm not even directly under this room and I could hear you."

"Can we talk about this once there aren't spiders?" I asked.

Chase sighed. "You two go home, I'll deal with it. We've had this happen before. A nest hatches above a light and they all come pouring out."

I shivered, hoping my cottage was spared a similar fate.

Marla and I scurried out the door. I brushed off my arms even though I hadn't been below the spiders. I felt like they were all over me.

"Well, that was a waste of time," I said as we walked across the hallway and down the stairs.

When we got to the bottom, there was a man about seventy standing there. He glared at me through his black-rimmed glasses.

"Are you the new owner?" he demanded.

"Yes, I'm Harmony."

He sniffed and glared at me. "There's a lot of commotion going on above my room."

"This is Sherman Bradley," Marla explained. "He lives under the room we were just in."

"Nice to meet you, Mr. Bradley," I said. "Sorry about the noise. We were working on some things."

"It's a little late for that, but at least it was you and not the ghost."

"You hear a ghost?"

He shrugged. "I hear something. Usually just footsteps at night and things falling. Sometimes the television. Nothing like tonight, though. I was a little worried."

"A nest of spiders hatched up there," I told him.

"That was a lot of commotion for spiders."

I just smiled. Explaining our purpose wasn't important right now.

Marla and I went our separate ways after reassuring Mr. Bradley there would be no further disturbance, and I ended up in my cozy bed with Samson cuddled up next to me.

I still kept itching my head every time I thought of the spiders, though, and I was probably going to have nightmares.

"Are you scared of spiders?" I asked Samson. "I bet you aren't. My parents were allergic to dogs, so I never had one. It would probably be smart to get a book on how to care for dogs, but I figure Chase knows what he's doing. I wish I could take you into the hotel."

Samson yawned, and I gagged. "That's some nasty breath, buddy. What do we do about that?" I wondered if most people talked to their dogs like they were going to answer. I was glad Samson was here. If he weren't, I would probably be talking to myself.

The next morning, I woke up early and went back to room 202. I put my hand on the doorknob, ready to go in.

"I wouldn't," Chase said from behind me.

I spun around. "Wouldn't what?"

"Go in there. I sprayed some pesticides in there to get rid of the spiders. It's harmless, but I still think people should stay out for a day or two."

I wrinkled my nose. I really wanted to search the room.

He crossed his arms over his black T-shirt. "What happened to the bed? And the picture?"

I wasn't sure what to say. Did I need to explain myself? It was my hotel, after all. Still, Chase's gaze made me feel like a little kid caught with their hand in the cookie jar.

"The picture was doing something weird, and when I tried to move it, it fell. Then I jumped on the bed to see what was going on with the light, and it appears the bed wasn't up for that type of abuse."

Chase's eyes sparkled, and I was almost sure he held in a smile. "The picture was doing something weird?"

"Yeah, it was moving from side to side. I know it's not a ghost, and I'm going to figure out what's going on."

"People want to think it's haunted. It doesn't matter what happens. They're going to keep believing it's haunted."

"Do you think it is?"

He shrugged, his gaze still fixed on me.

It made me want to fidget. I couldn't figure out what my weird obsession with this man was. I tried again to imagine what he would look like without a beard.

"I'm going to get to the bottom of it. There has to be an explanation as to why weird things happen there."

"Good luck with that. I hope you can do it without destroying the place."

"I own it, so I guess it's my problem."

He raised his brow and turned and took a few steps, then stopped. "The stew was good."

"I'm glad you liked it."

"I'm hard to find sometimes, so whatever you bring, you can leave in the fridge or on the stove."

"Alright."

He disappeared down the hallway.

I stared at the place he had been for a minute after he was gone. Chase Jensen was not the type of guy I should be getting obsessed with. He looked like someone who might live under a bridge.

That wasn't fair. He was clean, and he wore nice clothes.

Chase's captivating eyes were definitely stealing more of my attention than they should. He wasn't usually what I looked for. Talking was important to me, but getting conversation out of him wasn't easy.

My dating life had always been a mess. If I like a guy, you could guarantee he wouldn't like me. If a guy liked me, you better believe he was odd. That must've said something about me. I'd always wondered why I couldn't—for once in my life—like someone who liked me.

I took Chase as someone who didn't date, since he seemed to be hiding from the world, and even if he did, he probably thought I was crazy. And he might be a killer...

The 202 marking the door taunted me, and I sighed. I would stay out. But just for the day.

Samantha came around the corner with her cleaning cart. She had pulled her black hair into a braid today. Her eyes were wide, and her lips were pressed together as she spotted me.

"Hi, Samantha," I said. "Are you alright?"

"Yes. I just saw Chase Jensen. He was smiling. I've never seen that before. It makes me nervous."

My mouth turned up. "Because he smiled?"

She nodded. "I've never seen him smile. He must be up to something. Thanks again for cleaning that room."

"Sure."

"I can't believe it doesn't scare you."

"I'm sure there's an explanation for all of it."

"Well, I hope you figure it out. I can't walk past it without holding my breath."

"Why hold your breath?"

"So I don't get bad luck."

I bobbed my head. Being superstitious must be hard.

Chapter 5

My tongue rested at the side of my mouth while I carefully drizzled caramel over a piece of cheesecake.

Culinary school had made me realize that although I loved cooking, I didn't like cooking what someone else told me to. I like doing my own thing.

I placed the cheesecake on a tray with the other pieces I'd already decorated, and pride swelled in my chest. They looked perfect.

A knock on the door made Samson bark.

"It's alright, Samson," I said, answering it.

The sight of the sheriff greeted me. At least, that was what I assumed from the star on his tan button-up shirt.

"Can I help you?" I asked.

He took off his sunglasses and smiled. He looked a little older than me and had sandy blond hair and bright green eyes. His shoulders were as impressive as Chase's, and I felt a slight flutter in my stomach. The sheriff was attractive.

"I'm Sheriff Troy McGregor," he said, holding out his hand. "You must be Harmony Landing?"

I took his hand and nodded. "I'm Harmony."

"Nice to meet you."

Samson barked and ran around the sheriff's legs.

"Hey, buddy," the sheriff said, rubbing behind the dog's ears.

Samson wagged his tail and barked again.

"I can't play right now. I'm on duty."

Samson whined.

"I didn't bring my frisbee."

Samson licked his hand.

"Great, now he's making me feel guilty. I'm actually looking for Chase Jensen, but I can't seem to find him. Do you know where he might be?"

I frowned as I wondered what the sheriff could want with Chase. "He's building something in my backyard. I'll take you to him."

I hoped this was only a social call. Marla had told me the sheriff and Chase were friends.

"Come, Samson," the sheriff said. The dog was more than happy to follow.

I closed the door and led him around the cottage. "I didn't realize you knew Samson," I said.

"Me and Samson go way back, don't we?"

Samson barked in what must be agreement.

Chase was sitting in the dirt, messing with some chicken wire. I'd decided that if I was going to sell food in the hotel, I wanted chickens, so I could have fresh eggs. Chase had looked at me like I was crazy, but he'd gotten right to work on a coop.

Chase frowned when he saw the sheriff. "What's going on, Troy?"

"Same as always."

Chase sighed and stood. "I've been here all day. All yesterday too."

Samson ran to Chase and licked his hand. That was one habit I couldn't get used to. Every time Samson licked my hand, I felt like I needed to wash it.

"I know, but I have to do my job."

"Yeah, I suppose."

"Someone crashed into the dumpster at Frizzle's Cafe and drove away last night. Someone said they thought they saw your truck peel out of the parking lot."

Chase wiped the sweat from his brow. "Seriously? Now I'm getting blamed for stuff like that? Doesn't the cafe have cameras?"

The sheriff shook his head. "No, but they're going to put some up."

"This is ridiculous."

"I know. I just had to come talk to you, so I have it in my report."

"I didn't do it," he said.

"Do you have anyone to vouch for you?"

Chase rubbed Samson's head. "What time was it?"

"About eleven."

"I was with him," I said.

The sheriff raised his eyebrow and smiled at Chase. "At eleven at night?"

"Don't be an idiot, Troy," Chase said, glaring at the man. "There was a spider problem at the hotel. Marla can vouch as well."

"Alright," the sheriff said. "You know, people would stop pinning everything on you if you tried harder." He didn't seem to mind being called an idiot.

Chase growled. "It wouldn't make a difference. I get blamed for everything in this town. If people really knew what my life was like, they would be bored to death. I know I am."

"You can change things, man. I can help you."

"It won't matter."

"You look like you just escaped from Azkaban. Shave and cut your hair. At least trim it so it's even. And don't glare at everyone."

Chase's eyes narrowed. "Don't you get tired of this conversation?"

"Yep, but I'm not giving up on you." He turned to me. "It was nice to meet you, Harmony."

"Do you want to come to the hotel and have some cheesecake?" I offered. "I'm just about to take some up for all the employees, and I could use a hand carrying one of the trays."

The sheriff grinned. "That sounds great. I haven't had cheesecake in a long time."

"I'll help too," Chase said. "I need a break."

I was surprised, but I led them both to the kitchen, and they both picked up trays of cheesecake, then followed me back to the hotel.

We went into the break room, and I texted all the employees, letting them know they could come get some when they had a minute.

The sheriff and Chase sat at a small round table and began eating their cheesecake. I wondered how Chase could eat without getting mustache hair in his mouth.

It hadn't been a full day since Chase told me I should stay out of room 202, but it was evening, so it had probably been long enough.

I took the elevator and found myself in the room once again. My eyes traveled over the ceiling and walls. No spiders. That was a relief.

Whatever Chase had done must have worked. He'd also rehung the painting. It was still cracked on the edge, but not bad enough to toss it. The bed I'd jumped on was still broken, though.

Closing my eyes, I listened, but I didn't hear any ticking or anything but the sounds of people in the hall.

Walking around the perimeter of the room, I knocked on all the walls just to see if anything seemed off. It all sounded the same.

The door opened, and Marla poked her head in.

"Hey, hon. I thought I might find you here. Anymore spiders?"

"Nope. I'm thinking of tearing out the floor just to see if anything is weird."

"Might as well," she said, coming in and shutting the door behind her. "You should cut a hole in the wall behind the picture to see if there's something behind it."

"Good idea. I wonder if I can get Chase to help."

"Chase sure talks to you more than I've ever seen him talk to anyone besides the sheriff."

"He barely talks to me."

"Perhaps, but it's still more than anyone else."

"And you said he's friends with the sheriff?"

"They were football buddies in high school or something like that."

"Hmm." I got on my hands and knees and looked under the bed that was still standing. The carpet looked funny. I pulled on it and it partially came up. "Hey, I might have found something."

Marla sank to her knees beside me. "What is it?"

"The carpet pulls up. There isn't enough space to see well." I stood. "We should move the bed and—"

Someone turned the doorknob.

"Quick, in the closet," I whispered. I jumped in, and Marla joined me.

"Why are we hiding?" Marla whispered.

I just put a finger to my mouth and tried to see out the small slats on the door. Light shined in through the slats, but I couldn't see out.

"I don't know what happened," Chase's voice said.

I frowned. He wasn't the one I wanted to come in. I'd been hoping it was someone coming to mess with the room and we would be able to catch them.

"She wants to figure out why people think this room is haunted."

The sheriff laughed. "That's funny. Tell her I've searched the entire thing and there's nothing interesting here."

Great. They were talking about me.

"She jumped on the bed and busted it, and threw a painting on the floor. You should have seen how guilty she looked when I came in."

I frowned, and Marla snickered.

"I think dealing with Harmony Landing is going to be a lot better than dealing with your aunt," the sheriff said.

"My aunt wasn't hard to deal with."

"No, but she wasn't entertaining or hot, either."

Chase chuckled. "Already developing a crush on the new owner?"

"Hey, I saw you watching her."

"That's because she was talking."

"Don't give me that. You haven't politely listened to anyone since—"

"I don't want to talk about that," Chase said. "Are we going to play?"

"Are you ready to lose?"

"You wish."

I looked at Marla's dim outline, and she shrugged.

A drawer opened, and I heard them rummaging around.

"You have to admit she's good-looking," the sheriff said. My face felt warm, and Marla poked me and shook with silent laughter. "She's got that shiny auburn hair and sparkling green eyes—"

"They're hazel, not green," Chase said.

"What does hazel mean anyway? I've heard people say hazel when they have brown eyes."

"They have some green and some brown. Maybe a little gold."

"Dang. You must be looking close," he teased.

"I'm not blind," Chase said.

"So you've noticed her?"

"I work with her."

"And you admit she's hot?"

"So she's hot, who cares?"

"So, you aren't interested?"

There was more noise, and the TV turned on.

"Are you serious?" Chase asked. "No woman is going to settle for me."

"They might if you looked more presentable. You used to have quite the following of female admirers. McKenzie would still take you. So would Quincy."

"Everyone thinks I do horrible things. How I look doesn't matter. And you know how I've always felt about McKenzie and Quincy."

"Well, if you aren't interested, do you mind if I ask her out?"

"McKenzie or Quincy? You can have them both."

"No, Harmony."

This was so embarrassing. It wouldn't be half as bad if Marla wasn't here shaking with silent laughter.

"She just got here. Let her get settled," Chase said.

"Uh-huh. I thought you might say something like that."

"I'm not making any plans with Harmony," Chase said. "She probably hates me. The first time I saw her, I slammed the door in her face."

"Why?"

"You know I've always wanted this hotel. I had the down payment saved, and Aunt Cathy wouldn't sell it to me. She said I was too young and my reputation would ruin it. I expected the new owner to be a grumpy old man. When I saw her standing there looking all—"

"Hot?" the sheriff offered.

"I was going to say young. It made me mad."

"Maybe she'll hate it here and sell to you."

"No. She's going to stay. I can tell."

"Well, I hope she does."

They must have sat on the bed because there was a creak.

"I've heard the rumors," Chase said. "It makes me wonder about Harmony. You know she's had to have heard something about me. She should avoid me, but she doesn't."

"I doubt many people believe the rumors. People just like to speculate. Everyone who knew you well believed you."

"But she didn't know me, and she's fine with letting me drive her around. That's not smart. I could be what everyone says."

I frowned.

"But you're not."

"No, but she doesn't know that."

Great. He thought I had no common sense. He was probably right.

The next half hour we spent trying to keep quiet while they played some type of fighting game on the TV. I didn't even know we offered video games at the hotel.

"Dude! You went down!" the sheriff said.

"Oh, man!" Chase said, laughing.

The sound of his laughter made my heart skip a beat.

"I should have seen that coming. You're so predictable," Chase said.

"Bam! Wack! Whoa!"

"Ha! There's more where that came from!"

I smiled. Chase sounded like any other guy playing video games.

Just when I thought I couldn't take it anymore, the sheriff said he needed to go, and they put away the controllers, which I assumed were kept in the drawers. We heard the door open and close.

We waited a minute to make sure they were gone.

I walked out of the closet with Marla right behind me.

"I'm too old for that," she said, stretching her back.

"It's good the sheriff had things to do," I said, shaking my head. "I thought we might be there for hours."

"Chase is sure different around the sheriff. He seemed normal for once." She paused and grinned. "And it sounds like the sheriff has his eye on you."

I waved my hand in dismissal. "He only met me today." The sheriff was nice and attractive, but I really hoped he wouldn't ask me out.

Marla laughed. "I was glad to not be you in there. At least they were saying good things about you."

"And now I know why Chase is grumpy with me. He wanted the hotel."

"He's grumpy to everyone, honey. Don't take it personally." She patted my shoulder.

"I'm just glad they left before they found out we were here. So, should we pull up the carpet?"

"I need to get back to the front desk. Anna probably thinks I've abandoned her."

"Alright. I might wait until tomorrow then. Today has felt like a long day."

Chapter 6

"Mr. Bradley asked if you would go talk to him if you came in today," Marla told me the next morning.

The moving van had come with all my things, and I had come to find Chase to see if he could give me a hand. I wasn't sure what his actual job description was, but everyone seemed to think he did everything.

"Who is Mr. Bradley again?" I asked.

"Sherman Bradley? He lives under room 202?"

"Oh. Right, I met him. I'm so bad with names. I'll go talk to him."

I sought out room 102. It was right next door to Chase's room. I knocked and waited.

The door opened, and Mr. Bradey poked his head out. "It's about time, Miss Landing. I've been waiting for over an hour."

"Did you not get my phone number? I sent it to all the residents."

"I have it, but I left a message at the front."

"I'm sorry, I just got here. If you text me, I can help quicker."

"Well, come in."

I entered, and my eyes went wide. Sherman's suite didn't look like any of the others I'd seen. He must have brought his own furniture. A king-sized bed sat in the center of the room. It had a shiny blue comforter and matching pillows. A leather sofa rested against the foot of the bed, putting it close to the dresser. If he watched TV in here, it would only put him a few feet away.

He had also replaced the kitchen appliances. They were stainless steel and a nicer brand than the hotel carried. The carpet was thick and gray, and the room didn't smell like the rest of the hotel. That gave me hope for the guest rooms. Maybe changing the carpet would fix the smell.

"What can I do for you?" I asked.

"There has been a lot of noise coming from the room above. I require silence. It's almost as bad as when there used to be a person living above me."

"It is a hotel," I reasoned. "I don't think it was built to block out sound."

"I pay a lot of money to live here, and I need quiet."

"I've been working in there. I'll try to be quieter."

"I wish you would."

"You said you've never heard a ticking sound in your ceiling?"

"No, but I can't hear things like that," he said, pointing to his hearing aid. "I've enjoyed living here since they stopped putting people in that room above, and I hope I can keep enjoying it. I would hate to have to move."

"That would be a shame," I said. In reality, it wouldn't bother me. From the reports I'd been over, the hotel was almost always bringing in a good amount of money. If he left, I didn't think it would hurt any finances.

"I don't mind a little noise if it's before six in the evening. Anything after that is a nuisance."

"I'll keep that in mind," I said.

I told him goodbye and went next door to see if Chase was home. He wasn't, so I went back to my cottage and began unloading the truck. I didn't bring a lot, but some of it was big and awkward. The cottage had come with a bed, but it would be nice to have my own. I wasn't sure what to do with the one that was already here.

I unloaded the smaller things first, since they were the closest to the door. Once those boxes were all in, I stared at my couch, chair, washer and dryer, and bed. Chase's aunt had left a table and chairs, so I'd given mine to my parents, which would make it a little easier.

Grabbing my big stuffed chair, I pulled. It made a horrible noise as it dragged against the metal floor of the truck. I cringed and tried to lift it so it wouldn't scrape.

With effort, I got it out of the truck and dragged it across the grass while Samson ran around my legs. I took a deep breath and sighed. The couch was going to be impossible without help, and I didn't even want to think about the washer and dryer.

"I don't suppose you can help me lift?" I asked Samson.

He tilted his head and stared at me.

"Yeah, I didn't think so. I'm not going to get anything done here alone. You hold down the fort while I go tear out the carpet in room 202."

I grabbed a pry bar and a hammer and went to the hotel. The halls were full of people in swimming suits, as usual. We were close enough to the beach that most people just walked over. A reminder that I needed to make the trip myself at some point.

I made my way to the room and pushed open the door. Sherman couldn't complain about any noise I might make. It was much earlier than six.

The bed wasn't hard to move, so I pushed it as close to the wall as I could, and I grabbed the loose piece of carpet. I pulled and cringed at the sound of tearing. I hadn't pulled very hard, but the carpet must be rotting.

This was ridiculous. I would redo this entire room when I finished, so ruining things wouldn't matter.

Tearing up the carpet from that area only took a few minutes. The padding was so thin I couldn't imagine it was doing any good, and some of it had disintegrated into a messy yellow powder.

I cocked my head when I revealed the floor underneath. Old wooden planks stared up at me. My guess was that it was the original flooring. It was dusty but looked solid.

I'd thought there would be a trapdoor or loose planks, but it appeared I wasn't that lucky.

The pry bar didn't have anywhere to slip under since there were no cracks, so I held it up and used everything in me to smash the sharper side between the boards. I managed to dent it, but nothing too impressive. Then I took the hammer and hit the same place over and over until I'd made a good-sized hole in the floor.

"Sorry, Sherman," I muttered as I grabbed the pry bar and stuck it into the hole I made.

The wood cracked as I pushed on the bar. I pulled a big chunk of the floor off and tossed it to the side. What I was expecting, I don't know, but all that was under the floor were support boards. My mouth turned down, and then the ticking began.

The sound was coming from the floor to the right of where I'd ruined it. It was under the broken bed.

I pushed the bed out of the way and pulled more carpet back and glared when I saw a small square cut into the wooden boards. The carpet even had a loose piece of carpet shaped like a square that had been placed over the small trapdoor. I wouldn't have needed to tear the carpet if I'd been more thorough in my search.

I pried back the door and smiled when I looked inside. There was a box, no bigger than seven inches either way, and in the box was a clock.

My hands wrapped around the small clock as I inspected it. It was only about five inches around and wasn't ticking at the moment.

"Hello in there," said an unfamiliar man's voice.

I dropped the clock and put a hand to my heart. "Hello?" I said, ignoring my pounding heart.

A man in his mid-sixties entered, glancing at the mess I'd made. He had brown and gray hair and was probably about as tall as me, maybe five foot seven.

"I'm Harvey Vaughn. I live upstairs."

I grabbed the clock and stood. "I'm Harmony."

"The woman who bought the hotel?"

"Yes."

"I've been hearing more noise than usual from down here today, so I was just curious to know what was happening. A remodel?"

I nodded. "I figure it's time."

He glanced at the clock in my hands. "I think it's been time for a while. You're even tearing up the floors?"

"Just in here. The floors under the carpet are still solid. Well, except where I tore it up. I do want to get new carpet everywhere. It might help with the smell."

"That would be nice. My room smells like me, so it covers up the musty smell, but I wouldn't mind new carpet. Where did you get that clock?"

"It was in the floor." I gestured to the mess.

His wiry brows rose. "In the floor? Interesting. I hear a clock tick several times a day. I wonder if there's one in my floor."

I tapped my fingers against the clock. "Hmm. I wouldn't be surprised. I heard a tick from the ceiling the other day. We can check if you want. I think someone must have placed them to make people think this room is haunted."

Harvey chuckled. "I wouldn't doubt it. Some people like thinking this room has a ghost. I tell them that's baloney, but they believe it anyway."

"It would be easy to put a clock in this room since no one uses it. It would have been harder to sneak one into your room. And how do they make it tick at certain times?"

Harvey rubbed his chin. "That is curious. Some days it doesn't tick at all, other days I hear it several times."

The door opened, and Chase entered. "What's going on in here? Sherman said it sounds like the ceiling is going to fall on him. You're tearing up the floor?"

I handed him the clock. "I found this in the floor."

Chase turned it around and studied it. "Well, that explains some things. It's not ticking."

"It must have a remote, or some type of timer," I said. "I bet there's one in the ceiling and in the walls. I've heard ticking from all those places."

"If someone has a remote, then they're still messing with people. It's not just a quick prank. It has to be someone nearby."

"Why would anyone want people to think it was haunted?" Harvey asked. "How does it benefit anyone?"

Chase shrugged. "I'm going to text Troy. He shouldn't be far. We were just unloading your moving truck." He took out his phone and sent a message.

I tilted my head. "You unloaded my truck?"

"Yeah. You ruined part of your lawn dragging something across it. We thought you might need help."

"I'm going to go get my hat, then I'll be back," Harvey said, leaving the room.

I tilted my head and watched him go. "Why does he need a hat?"

Chase shrugged and walked around, knocking on the walls. A few minutes later, the sheriff came in. Harvey was right behind him, wearing a hat that looked straight out of *Sherlock Holmes*.

"Hey, Troy," Chase said. "Harmony found a clock in the floor."

"What?" the sheriff asked as I handed him the clock. "How did I miss this? I searched this room so well when I was looking for leads."

Chase rubbed his beard. "Well, you did that before all the strange things began. The first time anyone heard anything weird was... a few months after Tessa died."

"So it happened after. We're going to have to tear this place apart," the sheriff said, looking at me.

"Whatever you need to do, Sheriff."

"Call me Troy," he said, flashing his white teeth.

Chase rolled his eyes. "Should we tear down all the walls? People have complained about sounds in the walls and the ceiling."

Troy tapped his lip as his eyes scanned the room. "We might need to."

Harvey was holding a magnifying glass and inspecting every inch of the room. I smiled. I was going to like Harvey.

"It's going to be expensive to fix something like this," Harvey said in a British accent.

I shrugged. "We don't use this room, so fixing it isn't a priority."

"The question I have is, was the person who did this just trying to be funny, or are they trying to keep people out?" Troy said. "It could be the same person who killed Tessa. It's always bothered me that we never found out who did it."

Harvey paused and looked at Chase.

Chase just scowled, and Harvey looked away.

Troy looked at the clock. "We shouldn't have touched the clock. It might have had prints on it."

I hadn't thought of that. "What do you want me to do? Help bust down walls?" I held up my hammer.

Troy grinned. "As fun as that sounds, I think I'd better do it."

"By yourself?"

"Chase can help me."

My mouth turned down. "Why can he help and not me? I can break a wall."

"Chase and I used to work together for a builder. We can do it without destroying everything, and make sure we don't hit a load-bearing wall." He looked at the mess I'd made of the floor.

"Well, I'm going to stay in here and watch."

"I don't think that's a good idea," Chase said.

"Why?"

He looked at Troy, and Troy shrugged.

"There must be something behind this picture," I said, pointing at the painting I'd dropped. "The picture was moving from side to side."

"Let's start there," Troy said. "We need better tools. I'll go get some and be back."

I turned to Harvey. "Hey, Harvey? Do you want to go up to your room, and we can see if there might be a loose spot of carpet under your bed? If it's like the one down here, it would be easier to look under the floor than in the ceiling."

"That's a good idea," Harvey said, still using his accent. "Let's go."

We went up a floor in the elevator and into Harvey's room. His bed had a comforter covered in pictures of trout, and he had a singing fish mounted on the wall.

I hid a smile. I guess everyone has their own style. His room was a lot different from Sherman's.

"You like to fish?" I asked.

"Yep. Best way to relax."

"Let's move your bed and see what's under there."

His bed was heavier than the one downstairs, probably because it wasn't a hotel bed. We got it out of the way and studied the floor.

"I don't see anything," I said. "The carpet is tight. We might have to look in the ceiling downstairs."

Harvey nodded. "I'm relieved, in a way. It means no one has been inside my room. That would make me nervous."

Chapter 7

Troy decided he needed to get a saw so they could cut the walls neatly. I would have been happy to bash the walls with a hammer, but I would let the sheriff do his thing. He'd come back tomorrow when he had more time.

The next day, I wanted to go check on Chase and Troy's progress in room 202, but Sherman caught me while I waited for the elevator.

"There's a lot of noise going on above me," he said, adjusting his glasses. "I'm too old to be disturbed like this."

"Sorry," I said. "There's a police investigation going on up there, so you're going to have to deal with it for a while."

"A police investigation? Why?"

I just shrugged. I didn't feel like explaining anything to him.

"I've had a few years of peace and quiet, and now noise again."

"The woman who lived above you was loud?"

He rolled his eyes. "So loud. It's a pity she went out the way she did, but it's made my life better. She used to have people over at all hours of the day and night. And the music? Oi, the music. I complained about her every other day, but she didn't seem to care. She'd be quiet for a minute, then the noise again."

I nodded and tried to look sympathetic. I felt bad for whoever usually had to listen to his complaints every day. Still, someone constantly making noise would be irritating.

"I started complaining to her personally, but she wasn't a nice person."

"And she dated Chase Jensen?"

He laughed. "That would have been a mess. They never dated."

"Who was she dating when she died?"

"Who wasn't she dating? I don't think she had a boyfriend."

"The news said that she'd argued with her boyfriend."

He nodded. "That was a mistake. She argued with Chase. They argued all the time, but they didn't date. The news got it all wrong."

"What did they argue about?"

"He was the one who always went to tell her to be quiet when I complained. She didn't like him because he didn't think the world revolved around her like so many others. I guess she had a thing for him in high school, but he shut her down." The older man shook his head. "It's too bad everyone blames him."

"You don't?"

"Nah. He's not the type. Although Tessa could drive the most sane man crazy. There were tons of people who had bad experiences with her, but for some reason, everyone wants to think Chase did it. Chase used to be so lively. He still comes over for a game of checkers every once in a while. It's sad how fast a town can turn on a person."

"So Tessa had a lot of enemies?"

"Tons. You can't date every guy in town and dump them and not make enemies. It's also not a good way to make women friends. There are so many people who hated her, it would be impossible to find them all for questioning."

"Hey, Uncle Sherman," a man said, walking up to us. He looked about thirty, with dark brown hair and eyes. "Who am I yelling at today?"

Sherman cocked his head and let out a long breath. "You act like it's a regular occurrence."

"It is."

"This is Harmony Landing. She owns the hotel. Harmony, this is my nephew, Zack Bradley."

"Nice to meet you. Could I have a minute?" Zack asked me.

"Sure."

"I'm going back to my room," Sherman said, ambling down the hall. "Tell her about my rules."

"Sorry about my uncle," Zack said. "He's never been a ray of sunshine."

I waved a hand. "He's fine."

"Sherman's pretty irritated by all the noise above his room the last week or so."

"I know. I can't do anything about it. There's a police investigation going on in the room above."

Zack twitched slightly. "Oh? Something new happened there?"

"No, it's old stuff."

He rubbed his lips together and looked at the ceiling. "I thought that case was pretty much closed."

"I found something in there that might help the police."

He swallowed. "Oh. Great. Maybe they'll finally put the pieces together."

"Maybe."

"So, Sherman's going to have to deal with noises for a while. Could he be temporarily moved to another room? He's so annoying when he gets disturbed."

"If he wants to."

He nodded. "I'll talk to him and see what he thinks."

"Great. Let me know. I'm surprised Sherman doesn't get an apartment. I can't imagine living in a hotel room."

"He's odd that way. I tried to get him to at least go to a place with meals, but this is where he wants to be. He likes to eat out."

"And you take care of all his annoyances?"

"Yeah. If you don't obey Uncle Sherman, you don't get a monthly allowance. It sounds terrible, I know, but I have lots of expenses."

I wouldn't judge someone for getting money they didn't earn. I wouldn't have been able to buy this place without the money I'd inherited.

"Good luck with your uncle."

"Thanks." He nodded and walked down the hall toward Sherman's room.

I pushed the elevator button and tried to gather all my thoughts. They were moving through my head so fast I wasn't sure where to focus.

My mouth dropped when I walked into room 202.

Two of the walls were almost completely torn down. Chase and Troy were sitting on the floor playing a video game. They both looked guilty when I smiled at them.

"Working hard?" I asked.

"We were just taking a quick break," Troy said, turning off the game.

"I'm not judging. I have a theory about who killed Tessa."

"Let's hear it," Troy said, standing.

"I think it was Sherman, or possibly his nephew, Zack."

Chase stood. "Why them?"

"Sherman hates all the noise, and Zack doesn't get a monthly allowance if Sherman isn't happy with him."

Troy rubbed his chin. "Hmm. Sherman was always complaining about Tessa."

"He just told me his life was better after she was gone."

Chase nodded. "So were a lot of people's. That doesn't make him guilty over everyone else she annoyed."

"Yes, but what if he killed her, then did weird stuff to the room so no one else would stay there and bother him?"

"It's possible," Troy said.

"Did you find anything inside the walls?"

"Yep. There was something behind the painting rigged to make it move. It was on a timer. We also found another clock in the ceiling and two more in the walls. The clocks all work with a remote and a timer, which makes me think it's someone nearby."

"Like Sherman?"

"Possibly."

"Sherman wears me out," Chase said. "He complains more than anyone I know. Ninety-eight of one hundred complaints at the hotel are from him."

"That reminds me," I said. "Who is the hotel manager? I can't find it in any of the papers."

"That's because my aunt didn't have a manager. I did all that stuff."

"Oh. Are you still doing it?"

"Yep."

"I hope I pay you a lot. You're doing, like, three people's jobs."

He shrugged. "I learned this business as a kid."

I nodded and felt a little guilty about buying the hotel when he'd wanted it. "Did your parents live here?" I asked.

"My parents are irresponsible," he said. "My aunt raised me in your cottage."

My eyes went wide. "Did I kick you out of your home?"

"No. I moved to the hotel years ago. I needed my own space once I wasn't a kid. My aunt is great, but she can be a little smothering."

I felt a little better, but not much. This hotel should be Chase's.

"Chase wanted to buy this place," Troy said.

"Oh, really?" I had to pretend I didn't know or they would find out I'd been spying on them, which was embarrassing, even if it was unintentional.

"His aunt knew she owed it to him. He's done so much work for her over the years, but she's stubborn."

"Let's not go there," Chase said.

"Do you want to buy half of it from me?" I hadn't expected to say that.

Chase's eyes narrowed. "What?"

"I spent almost all my money on this place, and it needs a lot of work. I don't have the money to redo it all, but if I could get a co-owner, I could remodel the entire thing."

Something sparked in Chase's eyes, but I couldn't tell what.

"But if you had a co-owner, you would have to agree with them on everything," he said.

"Are you saying you're disagreeable?"

His eyes glistened. "Occasionally."

"Well, what if I keep fifty-one percent and you buy forty-nine percent?"

"Or we could do it the other way around."

I raised my eyebrow. "You think I'm going to give you more control?"

He stepped closer to me. "Fifty-fifty."

"So, we argue over all the decisions?"

His mouth twitched at the corner. "It might be fun."

"So you're interested?"

"I can't tell you how much."

I held out my hand, and he shook it. His eyes felt like they were staring into my soul. I couldn't look away, and I didn't want to. He had the loveliest brown eyes I'd ever seen.

"Wellll... should we get back to work?" Troy asked.

I pulled my hand away when I realized we had been standing there holding hands, staring at each other. Of course, we were doing it for different reasons. I was having weird romantic thoughts, and he was trying to see if I was serious about the hotel thing. I couldn't believe I was drawn to someone like Chase.

Troy grinned as he began cutting the wall. I wondered why. It seemed like he should be tired from all this work.

"How did the person who did this get the things behind the walls?" I wondered.

Chase grabbed a fallen piece of drywall and showed me the back of it. "The walls have been patched up. Someone cut pieces out and fixed it."

"And no one heard it? I would think Sherman would have complained."

"He complains so much, no one takes anything seriously."

"So he did complain?"

"It was five years ago. I can't remember."

Troy pulled back a piece of the wall. "They might have been able to do it quietly if they just sawed small pieces out."

I nodded. "Or it could have been Sherman, and no one else cared enough to complain."

"Everyone knew about the murder," Chase said. "And everyone knew we weren't renting out the room. Anyone could have gone in at their leisure and worked on this, and no one would interrupt."

"Except Sherman." I was really finding it hard to believe Sherman wouldn't have put up a lot of fuss if someone was doing this above his room."

"I'll talk to Sherman," Troy said. "See if he remembers anything. It was a long time ago, though, and he's complained so much, I doubt he'll remember a complaint from that far back."

"I'm going to go play with Samson if you don't need me," I said. "I don't think he's getting enough exercise."

"He loves frisbee," Chase said.

I wrinkled my nose. "Yeah, but he's not very good at it."

Troy chuckled. "What? Samson's great at frisbee."

"If you say so." I'd tried to play frisbee with Samson twice, and he only caught it once.

"Come on," Chase said. "I'll teach you."

"I don't think I need someone to show me how to throw a frisbee to a dog. It doesn't take skill or anything."

Troy grinned. "Let Chase show you. We used to be great at ultimate frisbee."

"Alright." I followed Chase from the room. I didn't think it would be helpful, but I wouldn't turn down an opportunity to spend more time with Chase.

We strolled over to the cottage, and Samson ran out when I opened the door.

I hurried in and grabbed a green frisbee from the top of the fridge and went back out. I've gotten into the bad habit of storing things up there.

"Throw it," Chase said. "Let me see how you're doing it."

Samson jumped up and down near me, waiting.

I flung it, and Samson took off after it. It hit the ground and rolled on its side. Samson picked it up in his mouth and brought it back.

I turned to Chase. "See? He hardly catches it."

I might not have been able to see Chase's mouth, but I could tell from his eyes he was smiling.

"You throw like—"

"Don't say it," I said.

He chuckled. "You throw like someone who doesn't know how to throw."

I crossed my arms. "You think you can do better?"

Chase took the frisbee from Samson and threw it. Samson ran after it, jumped in the air, and caught it in his mouth.

I shook my head. "Alright. You win. I'll have to find another way to help him get his exercise."

"I'll try to work with him more. I'll take him for a walk right now."

"Thanks."

"You don't have to thank me. I'm the one who should be taking care of him. He's not even your dog."

"I like helping, and I'm honestly glad he's here. Living alone is... lonely."

Chapter 8

I went back to my cottage to finish unpacking. The night before, I'd started but hadn't finished. I wasn't the type who could let boxes stay packed in the corner for weeks, so I was up half the night putting things away. I'd only taken a break to make dinner and run some over to Chase's room.

Samson was running around the cottage, barking at every new thing that came out of a box. His walk with Chase hadn't calmed him down, but his tail wagged, so I guessed it was happy barking.

Having a dog was fun, and I didn't have to deal with the annoying parts of it, thanks to Chase. I wondered how much I paid him. Probably not enough. If we really became business partners, I wasn't sure how all the money stuff would work.

I frowned. I wondered if Chase would want to hire a manager. He had to take care of all the gritty work, but he might not want to if he were part owner. That was something I needed to figure out, and soon. I couldn't let my hotel get run into the ground because I wasn't communicating right or aware of the finances.

Still, I doubted Chase would let it come to that. He knew what he was doing.

By the time the last box was empty, I felt exhausted. I fell into bed without changing out of my jeans, and sleep came for me.

At five in the morning, my eyes popped open.

Something had woken me, but I wasn't sure what. Samson was on the bed next to me, and he raised his head.

His ears perked up. It wasn't just me.

"Did you hear something?" I whispered.

A noise in the backyard made me freeze. I grabbed my phone and wondered what to do. I didn't want to call 911 if it was just an animal or the wind. It could be anything. I put the phone in my back pocket and pulled on my tennis shoes. I grabbed Samson's leash and hooked it to his bright blue collar.

I opened the front door carefully and went around the cottage.

Samson didn't want to sneak. He wanted to charge into the back with a vengeance. I tried to rein him in, but he dragged me.

When we got to the back, I turned on my phone flashlight, glanced around, and frowned. The chicken coop that Chase had been working on was destroyed. He'd been almost finished, and now it was torn to pieces. I couldn't believe someone could do this without me hearing.

Samson began barking and pulling on the leash. He was looking into the dark trees at the end of my property. There were several trees, and then the area was fenced along the property line. If someone was over there, they were stuck, unless they jumped the fence.

"No, Samson, stay," I commanded.

He broke free and ran.

I looked around frantically, trying to decide what to do. I didn't want to run into the dark, but I didn't want to lose Samson. "Samson!" I yelled. "Come back!"

I ran after him and tried to look at my phone at the same time. I managed to find Chase's number and pressed the button.

Samson ran back to me, grabbed my shirt in his mouth, and pulled me forward.

I almost dropped the phone. I would have to call later. I put the phone in my pocket and let the crazy dog drag me into the trees.

"Stop!" I commanded.

A shadowy figure ran from behind one tree and climbed the chain-link fence, throwing themselves over the top. The person hit the ground on the other side and stood and ran.

Samson released me and ran to the fence, jumping over it.

"Samson! No!" I yelled. I worried he would hurt himself with his leash flapping behind him. I climbed the fence and carefully jumped to the other side.

Samson was still in pursuit, and I couldn't see the figure. We ran through some more trees and then ended up on a dark sidewalk. Samson had a lead on me, but I could see the person running now.

"Samson!" I called again.

The person threw down a garbage can, and Samson jumped over it.

I jumped when I came to it, too, and sighed with relief when I cleared it. I probably should have gone around it, but I was in panic mode. I'd only known Samson for a few days and already loved the rascal.

"Come back!" I commanded.

Samson paused and looked at me, then at the figure who was racing away. He gave them one more glance, then came over to me.

"Not cool, Samson," I said, picking up his leash. We walked out to the main street because I didn't want to go over the fence again. The street here was lit up by all the restaurants lining the road.

When we got to the hotel, we walked around the back and to the cottage.

Samson barked, and Chase came running from behind the cottage. He stopped when he spotted us and wiped his brow. He dropped to his knees, and Samson pulled his leash from my hand again and ran to him. The dog barrelled into Chase and began licking him.

"What's going on?" Chase asked, rubbing the dog's head. "I got your call, but all I could hear was you yelling at Samson and panting. I saw the chicken coop."

I frowned. I must be really out of shape for him to hear my breathing through the phone.

"We heard something out back."

He tilted his head. "And you went out in the dark to see what it was?"

"I took Samson, but he broke away and chased after someone. He jumped the fence, and I went after him."

"I'm calling Troy." He already had his phone in his hand. He'd probably been listening to my entire dog chase, wondering what I was doing.

Samson came back to me and licked my hand. It took effort not to wipe it clean on something immediately.

"Hey, Troy," Chase said. "There was someone at Harmony's cottage messing with things. Yep. Bye." He reassured me, "He's coming."

I nodded. Chase definitely didn't waste words.

"Do you want to come in?" I asked.

He nodded, and we went in. I turned on the lights and motioned for him to sit. I smiled when I noticed he was still in his pajamas. He must have popped right up when I called and ran. I touched my hair. It was a mess. I was only dressed because I'd slept in my clothes.

Chase sat on my chair, and Samson rested his chin on Chase's knee.

I sat on the couch. "How far away is the sheriff?"

"He lives in town, so no more than five minutes."

We sat awkwardly until Troy knocked on the door.

I opened it, and he came in. He had bedhead but was dressed.

"What happened?" he asked through a yawn.

I told him the quick story.

"Never go outside to check on a noise," he scolded. "Call 911, or call me. Actually, call me. That saves you a step because I'll get the call eventually anyway. Give me your phone."

I handed it to him, and he put his number in the contacts.

Chase's eyes narrowed, and he crossed his arms.

"I'm going to go look out back and see if I can find anything. What did he look like?"

"I couldn't make out anything. I wouldn't even swear it was a man. They had dark clothing, and their hair was covered."

He looked at Chase. "You coming?"

Chase nodded, and they went out. Samson tagged along behind them.

I sighed. I hurried to the kitchen and pulled out the skillet. I plugged it in and let it heat while I mixed up pancake batter. While the first pancakes were cooking, I rushed to my room and ran a brush through my tangles.

By the time Chase and Troy came back, I had three stacks of pancakes on the table.

"I hope those are for us," Troy said.

"Yep. Sit down."

They both sat across from each other, and I sat at their side.

"Find anything?" I asked.

Troy poured syrup on his pancakes. "No. I can try to get someone to come check the coop for fingerprints. I'll look around some more after it's lighter."

The sun was beginning to shine through the crack in the curtains, and I yawned.

Chase took a bite and looked at Troy. "You know I'm going to get blamed for this."

"No one can blame you," I said. "You were here when we got back."

"People blame Chase for everything," Troy said. "It doesn't matter if it makes sense or not. I keep telling him he needs to change his image, but he doesn't listen."

Chase growled. "Shaving isn't going to make people trust me."

"But the way you hide behind your facial hair makes some people think you're up to something."

"I'm not hiding."

Troy raised his brow. "Oh no? It sure seems like it."

"Do we really have to talk about this now?" Chase asked, glancing at me.

Troy turned to me. "I keep telling him to shave and maybe get a girlfriend. If the townspeople saw him out with a respectable woman from the community, they might change their minds about him."

Chase snorted. "No respectable woman from the community is going to be seen with me."

"What about McKenzie? She thinks you're guilty, and she still likes you."

"Shouldn't that tell you something about her? I would rather everyone avoid me than go anywhere in public with McKenzie."

Troy stabbed his pancake and grinned. "Come on. Let a few people see you kissing some girl around town, the gossip will soon change."

"I don't know if you've noticed, but there isn't a group of women lined up at my door looking for a kiss."

"That's because they wouldn't be able to find your lips," I said, taking a sip of orange juice.

Troy burst into laughter. "She has a point."

Chase shook his head and rolled his muscular shoulders.

"If you like having a beard, that's one thing," Troy said. "At least trim it. Let the women all see you do have lips."

"It won't matter. People already have opinions. Unless someone finds the real killer, no one will accept me."

"So, let's find the real killer," I said.

They both looked at me, frowning.

"It's been over five years," Troy said. "We never found any kind of clue. It's been too long now."

"Hmm." I took a bite of my pancake. It was getting cold. "It's probably the same person who put the clocks in the room. There might be clues now that weren't there the first time you looked."

"That's very true," Troy said.

"I probably should trim my beard," Chase muttered. "I probably made myself look guilty when I grew it and became antisocial. It was like I was admitting something was wrong."

"At least make it even," I agreed.

"And cut your hair," Troy added.

"Lots of guys have long hair."

"Do you like it?"

"No, but I don't want to go to the barber and talk to Harold. He's as big a gossip as anyone I've ever seen."

"That's why you haven't cut it?" I asked. "I can do it."

He tilted his head and might have grinned. "Aren't you a beauty school dropout?"

My mouth turned down. "I wouldn't say dropout. I quit because I hated it."

"That would count as a dropout."

"Fine, but I can do it. Right now," I challenged.

Troy grinned. "I'm gonna watch."

"Don't you have a job?" Chase asked.

Troy laughed. "Yep, and it's in your hotel."

I got up and went into the bathroom. I'd put my hair cutting things in the drawer under the sink. I pulled them out and took them into the kitchen.

"Come sit on the stool," I said, pointing. I hoped the equipment wasn't rusty.

Chase groaned but did as he was told.

I took out my scissors. "I'm going to cut it shorter really fast before I use the clippers."

He nodded.

"You can close your eyes if you're scared."

Troy laughed again, and Chase fixed me with a glare. I cut it straight across the back and tossed the hair on his lap.

He frowned and brushed it to the floor.

The clippers were next. I turned them on and smiled mischievously at Chase. "Are you ready for this?"

"Just do it."

I hadn't cut anyone's hair in over five years, so I was surprised when it turned out even.

"I'm going to go look outside again," Troy said. "Try to get his beard now." He went out, and I smiled.

Chase ran a hand over the back of his head. "Wow, that feels weird. It's been a while."

"Should I trim your beard?"

He sighed. "Maybe a little."

"Ten inches?"

He raised his eyebrow. "Wouldn't that be the entire thing?"

I grinned. "Maybe."

"Do you know how ridiculous I would look? I'm pretty tan, and under this mess, I'm not. You can make it short, but don't take all of it."

I nodded and cut his beard right under his chin before he could change his mind. By the time I finished trimming the last strands, he had a short beard and a visible mouth. I tried not to stare at his lips when I tidied above them. He had nice lips.

"There," I said. "You can go look in the bathroom mirror if you want."

He shrugged. "I don't care about how I look."

I nodded. "Alright." I was going to be satisfied for now. I thought under all that hair Chase was going to be good-looking, and I was right. Facial hair isn't my thing, and I hoped someday I would see what he looked like without any of it.

Troy came back in. "Whoa! You almost look like you again. It's giving me flashbacks."

Chase rolled his eyes.

"You two went to school together and worked together?" I asked.

"Yeah," Troy said. "We've actually been best friends since we were five."

I nodded. It must be nice to have such a long friendship.

"We should get started at the hotel," Troy said. "Unless you want to go looking for girls, now you have lips again."

Chase stood and brushed hair from his shoulders, then ran over and put Troy in a headlock. "You better watch it."

Troy just laughed as he wiggled free.

"Shouldn't someone be looking for the man who was in my backyard?"

"I already have a few men on it," Troy said.

"Then let's go," Chase said. "We've given Sherman enough quiet for the morning."

I watched the two of them from the window as they walked up to the hotel. I probably shouldn't have given Chase a makeover. Now he was going to distract me more than he already did.

Chapter 9

My eyes locked on the door at the end of the hallway. If I wasn't seeing things, the door had just closed. The door went to the fire escape, and no one should be there.

Marla had told me that people snuck out there sometimes to smoke, but there was a sign by the door that read 'No Entrance Except in an Emergency.'

I slipped quietly to the door and opened it.

There was no one there. I stepped out onto the small cement landing and looked around. The fire escape was enclosed with bars and had metal stairs that went up and down since I was on the middle floor. I walked cautiously up and paused several times to listen. I had to step carefully so my shoes wouldn't make noise against the metal.

The stairs went up in a square. When I was almost at the top, I took a deep breath as I turned the last corner.

A scream bubbled up my throat as I turned and came face to face with Harvey, and I forced it down.

I wasn't the only one scared. He jumped when he saw me and dropped his magnifying glass.

"You scared the Dickens out of me," he said with a British accent. He reached down to retrieve it.

"Sorry," I said. "I saw someone go out and wondered what they were up to."

"I walk all around the hotel. That includes out here."

I nodded and looked through the bars. "Do you ever catch anyone up here?"

"Occasionally."

I noted the cement platform we were standing on. "It looks like the birds like it up here." The ground and the bars were a mess of bird droppings.

"They really do. I've tried to hang wind chimes and different things up to scare them away, but they don't seem to mind it."

"Are you the only security guard here?"

"Yep. I'm all we need."

"What about at night?"

"There's a night security number that people can call that comes to me. I also get up a few times to take a turn around."

"Have you ever noticed anyone hanging out near room 202?"

"No. We should probably have a camera pointed at the door. Probably should have cameras looking down all the halls. I tried to convince Cathy, but she said it ruins people's privacy."

"Do you like working here?"

He took off his deerstalker hat and itched his head. "It's pretty enjoyable," he said, his accent gone. "I retired early from the police force, then realized I wasn't made for a retirement kind of life. This gives me enough to do to be content."

"I'm going back to room 202 to look around some more. Do you want to come?"

He smiled and put his hat back on. "Of course I want to come, my dear." His accent was back.

"Does the hat affect your accent?"

He rubbed at an invisible mustache. "The hat makes the man. Now come. The game's afoot."

Harvey crawled across the floor of room 202, in the dark, shining his black light flashlight on the baseboards.

I stepped to the side, out of his way, and watched. Black lights should be banned. Everywhere he shined the light showed some sort of spill, and I was nervous now about the cleanliness of the hotel. How could it look clean and still show so much?

When we first came in, he showed me how the light worked in the bathroom. He'd flipped off the lights and shined the torch on the wall by the toilet. Glowing green streaks went down the wall. As soon as we were finished, I was going to get some bleach and scrub down all the walls.

"How does the black light work?" I asked.

"Elementary, my dear Harmony."

My mouth turned down, but I also felt amused.

"It emits ultraviolet light. We can't see it, but when it hits phosphors, they absorb the energy and re-emit it. It makes things glow under the black light."

I laughed softly. "You could just say you don't know. No need to make things up."

He chuckled. "I know more boring things than your average man. Don't ask me a question unless you want a boring answer."

The TV turned on and made me jump.

Harvey didn't seem phased. He just kept looking at the floorboards.

"Where's the remote?" I muttered, looking around the dark room.

The stations began changing, and I took a shaky breath. I knew there was nothing to fear. We already knew someone had rigged the room. Turning on the TV was probably an easy thing to do. I wondered if it could work from another floor, say, right below us.

I marched over to the TV and began feeling around for a button. I finally found one on the side and turned it off.

"That was freaky," I said.

"What was?" Harvey asked.

"The TV turning itself on."

"Oh. I thought you did that. Blast. I missed the chance of being scared."

I gave a small laugh. "You like to be scared?"

"Not too much, but a little adrenaline is good for you."

I rubbed the goosebumps on my arms. "I don't think it would have scared me if it weren't dark."

"I don't see anything out of the ordinary here. I'm sure it's been too long to find much."

The door opened, and the light flipped on.

Samantha stepped in and screamed when she saw us. The door slammed behind her, causing her to scream again. "What are you doing in the dark?" she asked, putting a hand to her chest. "I could have had a heart attack!"

Harvey stood up from behind the bed, and Samantha yelped.

"Sorry, Sammy," Harvey said. "We're looking for clues in here. Do you want to join us?"

Samantha shook her head. "This room gives me the creeps. I only came in because I noticed the window was open a crack when I drove up today."

I frowned and went to the window, pulling the curtains back. Sure enough, the window was open. I pulled it shut and locked it.

"You noticed that from your car?"

"The window used to open all the time. I got into the habit of looking for it when I came to work. It's been over a year since it happened."

"That's strange," Harvey said. "No one can do that with a remote. They would have to be in the room."

Samantha's eyes went wide.

"Don't worry," he said. "No one's here now. I already looked under all the beds and in the closet."

"I'm going to work now that the windows shut," she said, grabbing the doorknob. She fiddled with it for a minute. "It won't open."

I went and tried. The knob wouldn't turn.

"That's odd," I said as the TV turned back on.

Samantha crossed herself and pressed against the door.

"It's fine," I said, pulling the plug. "Someone's triggered things in this room to do weird things. Didn't someone tell you about the clocks in the floors and walls?"

"Yes, but what about the TV?"

"I'm sure someone has a remote somewhere."

"Stand back," Harvey said, motioning for Samantha to move. "I spent years of my life busting through doors."

Samantha moved, and Harvey twisted the doorknob a few times, then slammed the door with his shoulder.

"Ouch," he said, rubbing his shoulder.

I rolled my eyes. "The door opens inward."

"Right," he said, grinning sheepishly. "I was usually trying to bust a door in from the outside in, not from the inside out."

I went back to the window and pulled the curtains open wider. The sun streamed in, and I tried to see straight down. We weren't very high, but jumping seemed dramatic. I could probably beat on the floor, and Sherman would find someone to come see what was going on.

I opened the window and popped out the screen. Yelling down to someone would probably be faster.

"There is absolutely no one out there," I said, looking around. Everyone couldn't be at the beach. "I can see a ledge above the first-floor windows. I can probably lower myself to it, then I wouldn't be very high. I could even jump from the ledge."

"That sounds dangerous," Samantha said.

"No really, look," I said, pointing. "From the bottom of this window to the ground is only about twelve feet. The ledge above the lower window is about six inches wide. My feet can touch it from this window without me even having to drop to it."

"Someone will come looking for us eventually," Harvey said. "We can just sit and watch TV."

"But someone locked us in, and they must still be in the building or close by. We don't have time."

I climbed into the window and sat, dangling my legs over. Then I turned and lowered myself. Not gracefully, but within half a minute, I was hanging by my fingertips from the window.

Harvey and Samantha were looking out, frowning.

I moved my foot around until I found the ledge.

"Are you okay?" Harvey asked.

"Yes." I spun unhurriedly around, keeping one hand on the window ledge. The brick was rough against my hand. I was only four or five feet off the ground now. I let go and jumped carefully to the dirt below.

Smiling, I turned back to the window and gave them a thumbs up. My heart was pounding, but I was proud of myself. That had to have looked awesome.

"What do you think you're doing?" I heard Chase say.

I turned and saw Chase and Troy running toward me.

I tried to look innocent. "I was in room 202 with Harvey and Samantha, and someone locked us in. They're still up there."

Troy and Chase looked up, and Harvey waved.

"Come on," Troy said. We all rushed into the hotel. "Why did you go out the window?"

"Because I couldn't see anyone outside to yell at to help us. Harvey's too old to do it, and I'm sure Samantha would freak out."

Chase side-eyed me. "Why didn't you call someone?"

I pressed my lips together. The thought hadn't even crossed my mind.

"I want to say I didn't have my phone, but honestly, I panicked and didn't think about it."

We didn't wait for the elevator. We ran up the stairs. When we walked over to the room, we found a chair propped under the lock. Troy moved the chair and opened the door.

Samantha came rushing out, and Harvey wandered over.

"Why would someone trap us in a room?" I wondered. "I don't see a point."

"I'm going to look all over the hotel and have the outside cameras checked," said Troy, rushing off.

"It's always dangerous when you mess with the bad guys," Harvey said.

I shook my head. "But locking us in only puts us in the place they shouldn't want us to be." I looked at Chase. "The TV kept turning on when we were in there."

Chase rubbed his chin. "You can't use a TV remote from too far away. You usually have to be pointing at it."

"Unless they have a remote that uses radio frequencies," Harvey added. "Then they might be able to use it from another room."

"I'm out of here," Samantha said. "I'm going to do my job and mind my own business." She hurried in the same direction as Troy went.

"We need to check all the nearby rooms," I said.

Chase shook his head. "We can't just break into people's rooms."

"Well, it has to be Sherman, doesn't it? He's the only one who's close enough and has been here for long enough," I said. "Well, and Harvey, but he was with me, so we know it wasn't him."

"Sherman wouldn't be my guess," Harvey said. "He doesn't get around fast, and I doubt he has the skills to do something like this. He isn't the type to get his hands dirty."

"But he could easily use a remote from his room."

"He wouldn't have been able to stick the chair under the door and get to his room in that amount of time."

I blew out a breath. Sherman felt like the most obvious choice. No one else lived here, unless you counted Chase, and he'd been outside with Troy.

"Can't Troy fingerprint the chair?" I asked.

Chase shrugged. "Probably. I'm not sure it would be helpful, though. It's a lobby chair. Tons of people have touched it."

Chapter 10

Two days went by, and room 202 was completely torn apart. I stood in the room and watched Troy put the light fixture back up. All together, they had found five clocks and a few gadgets in the walls that moved pictures, but Troy hadn't figured out who had locked us in the room.

"I've been thinking," I said, turning to Chase, who was measuring for new drywall. "Should we really makeover this room? No one wants to stay in it, so it might be a waste of money we could use in another room."

"Your call," he said.

My mouth turned down. He hadn't mentioned anything about buying part of the hotel since that one conversation we had. I wondered if he changed his mind, and I didn't want to bring it up again. I didn't want to make big decisions without him if he was going to go into business with me.

"I thought about something else. Samantha said that she has to clean up garbage in here sometimes. Since no one stays here, there shouldn't be garbage. Is there an explanation for that? She also said the bathroom gets used."

"What type of garbage?" Troy asked.

"She didn't say. I can ask her."

"It's probably us," Chase said. "Troy and I come in here sometimes to play video games. I bet we've left some things a few times."

"Right," Troy said. "We do eat in here occasionally and put stuff in the trash. And we might use the bathroom."

"Well, that solves that," I said, not admitting I knew they used the room. I would never admit to overhearing that conversation.

"Why don't you play games in your own room?" I asked Chase.

Chase and Troy shared a guilty look.

"Because we microwave burritos in here and I don't want my room to stink."

I smiled and shook my head.

"It might be smart to redo the room," Chase said. "Now we have an explanation for the weird things happening, people will know it isn't haunted."

"True…" I agreed. "Hey, I've been thinking. Do you think people would be upset if we let Samson into the hotel? We could say he's part of the security."

"I would have to look into it. He isn't trained to be a guard dog. Some people might be upset to see an animal in a place that claims there are no animals."

"Can't we change that?"

"Do you really want a bunch of vacationers bringing their pets here? They might end up being left in rooms, tearing them apart, and who knows what else."

"That would be bad. What if we give him a sweater that says security or something? I think he's too bored."

"Let me think about it."

"Alright."

"I'm going to go see if the hardware store has any drywall. We should at least fix the walls." Chase stood and stretched. "I'll probably have to go somewhere else or order it. It's a small store." Chase left, and Troy jumped off his step ladder.

"You might fix Chase," he said bluntly.

I laughed. "Fix him?"

"Chase never goes to any of the businesses in town. I can't believe he just went. I think he's feeling more confident now that he doesn't look like a mountain man."

"I wonder why everyone blames him for Tessa's death. Nothing about him feels like a murderer."

"Chase is the best guy I know. He was always the first person to help anyone in town. It really shook him when people he grew up with started blaming him. There are plenty of people who don't blame him, but the ones who did broke him. He freaked and became as close to a hermit as you can get without being one."

"That's too bad. We need to solve that murder. Then he can go back to a normal life."

"That's not an easy thing."

"But it has to be possible."

"You're the first person who's taken an interest in helping Chase since it all happened. Well, besides me. I think that's helping him as well. Seeing that you don't judge him gives him more confidence. I'm not sure if he can tell you have a crush on him or not, but that won't hurt either."

All the color drained from my face. "I don't have a crush on him. I barely know him."

Troy smiled. "I didn't say you were in love with him. A crush can happen in a minute."

I put my hands on my hips. "You're crazy."

"Am I? I thought you were going to pull him in for a kiss the other day when you shook hands."

My eyes narrowed. "The thought never entered my mind."

"Okay, okay." He held up his arms in surrender. "Maybe I'm wrong, but you sure stare at him whenever he's around."

"That's because he's a mystery. I can't ignore a mystery."

"No mystery. I just told you why he's the way he is."

"Did he date a lot before it all happened?"

He raised his brow and smiled like I had just confirmed his suspicion. "Our high school was small, and somehow two-thirds of the population were girls. Chase and I thought that was the greatest thing that ever happened to us. Even the nerdiest guy had multiple girls asking him to every girl's choice dance. I know I don't have to say it, but Chase and I were not nerds, and we aren't too bad to look at."

I grinned slightly. "And you were humble, I'm sure."

He hooted. "Not at all. We loved having girls follow us around and compete for our attention. I'm embarrassed now, but we can't change the past. By the time senior year came around, there were a few popular girls who had threatened other girls to stay away from us. Unfortunately for us, they weren't people we wanted to be around."

"McKenzie? Her name seems to come up a lot."

"Yeah. McKenzie, Tessa, and Quincy. They were the main three. We tried to keep our distance, but those girls were persistent. Even after high school, they were out of control. Tessa kept getting into trouble, so her parents made her live at the hotel. They were tired of her friends at their house."

"High school was a long time ago," I said.

"Yeah, but it's a small town. It's hard to distance yourself from people. We kept hoping the three of them would leave town or get married. I threatened all three of them with a restraining order. Chase was nicer than me back in those days. That meant the three of them focused on him."

"McKenzie said she dated Chase."

"They went to *one* girls' choice dance. We both went to dances with all three of them, but never anything else."

"Who is Quincy? I've never met her. Is she still around?"

"Yep. She works at Betsy's Bagels. Her mom owns the place, Quincy runs it."

"So they all stayed in town?"

"Yep."

"Could Quincy or McKenzie have killed Tessa?"

He shrugged. "It's possible. I checked them closely when it first happened, but I never found anything to pursue. I will admit that was my first big case, and I'm not sure I did everything as well as I should have. There was a lot of stress, and I had a hard time thinking clearly."

Marla poked her head into the room. "Are y'all almost done in here?" She glanced around and frowned. "I guess not. Sherman's complaining again. He said it sounds like people are trying to disturb him."

"I'll go talk to him," Troy said. He squeezed past Marla and left.

Marla came in and studied the space. "When you tear apart a room, you really tear apart a room."

I laughed. "I didn't do it. It was Chase and Troy."

"Who is Troy—Sheriff McGregor?"

I nodded.

"I forgot he had a first name."

"Do you know where Betsy's Bagels is?"

Marla nodded. "Sure thing. You need directions, hon?"

"I was thinking of going there for lunch. Do you have a break coming up? I'd love for you to join me."

"My break just started, and I'd love to."

"Great."

"That sheriff isn't bad looking, is he?"

I laughed. "Not at all."

"You interested?"

"No. He's a nice guy, but not what I'm looking for."

Chase entered with a bag from the hardware store. "No drywall. I'll have to go into the city tomorrow."

"Can I go with you? Maybe I could look into getting a car."

"Sure. I'll leave tomorrow at nine."

"Great. Not being able to drive is a pain."

Chase's eyes twinkled. "I guess you shouldn't have been such a speed demon."

I grumbled. "I know. There was one cop who had it out for me. Everyone was always speeding, and he always stopped me. I was going with the flow of traffic. If I get a car, I won't be able to drive it home. I didn't think of that."

"Why get a car if you can't drive it?" Marla asked.

"I don't want Chase to have to put miles on his truck for me."

"I don't mind," Chase said. "It's not like anywhere around town is far." He grinned. "Maybe you can get a scooter. Then you could get around town and not need a license."

"Ha ha. Can I still go with you tomorrow? I don't think anyone can survive long on groceries from the store here. Those prices are insane."

"Yep. I go grocery shopping in the city every two weeks and stock up."

Marla winked at Chase. "Did you get a haircut? There's something different about you."

Chase laughed. "I guess I've been scaring people for long enough. Harmony hacked it off."

Marla raised her eyebrow. "Well, it suits you."

"Thanks."

"Are you ready?" I asked her.

"Yes. I just need to grab my purse at the desk."

We walked down the sidewalk, and I smiled. This place was growing on me quickly. The temperature always seemed perfect, never too hot, or too cold, and I would never tire of seeing palm trees.

"So, you aren't interested in the sheriff because you're interested in Chase Jensen? I can't believe he let you cut his hair."

"Why does everyone think I have something for Chase? You guys are all crazy."

Marla giggled. "Well, from the looks you were giving him, anyone might come to that conclusion."

I sighed. "Really? I've been trying to keep it to myself."

"I was right, then."

"Don't tell anyone. I don't know what it is about him..."

"He's a good guy. I hope things work for you."

"Nothing is going to happen between us. I think he's pretty set in his ways," I said.

"But people change. He's changing. I never would have expected that beard to shrink. And, we heard him admit he finds you attractive."

"Yeah, but I can be annoying. And I basically stole his hotel. There are lots of reasons he might not like me."

"Don't be hard on yourself. All of us are annoying in some way or another. Now tell me about what they found in the room. Any ghosts?"

I grinned. "No, but there were a bunch of clocks hidden in the walls. All of them can be controlled by a remote."

"How close does the remote have to be?"

"I'm not sure. I'd guess close."

"My money is on Sherman. I bet he did it so he doesn't have to deal with anyone living above him."

"I had the same thought. His nephew also gives me suspicious vibes."

We stopped in front of a cute little shop that was painted light pink. It had a big sign that said 'Betsy's Bagels.'

We went in and looked around. There were six round tables and a small counter with different pastries inside. Only two tables were occupied. We stepped up to the counter, and I looked inside to see my options.

We ordered bagels and sat at a table. The woman at the counter had a name tag, and she wasn't Quincy.

"These are good bagels," I said. "And they sell coffee here."

"You didn't get any coffee," Marla pointed out.

"I'm not a coffee drinker. The girl, Tessa? She died from poisoned coffee. I wonder if it came from this place."

"Is that why you chose this place?"

I nodded. "The manager had a thing for Chase. So did Tessa."

"You think she killed her?"

"No, I've never met her, but anything is possible. I would love to prove Chase innocent to all the people in this town."

"Mm-hmm," Marla said, tucking bright red hair behind her ear. "I'm willing to help."

A woman with long black hair came in and went behind the counter. She moved some things around and then looked around the shop. Her eyes stopped on us. She pushed her hair over her shoulder and came over to our table.

"Hello, I'm Quincy. You must be the new owner of Harmony Landing."

"Yes," I said, shaking her hand. "I'm Harmony."

"I recognized the receptionist. Sorry, I forgot your name." Her tone sounded disinterested when she spoke to her.

"Marla," Marla said.

"Right. Sorry." She turned back to me. "I hear they're opening Tessa's case again. Is that true?"

"Yes," I said. "There's been some new evidence."

Quincy tilted her head. "New? After all these years? What is it?"

"I'm not sure," I lied. I didn't want everyone to know all the details. "The sheriff is handling it all."

"I hope they clear Chase. He doesn't deserve all he's been through. Have you met Chase Jensen?"

I nodded. "I see him every day since we work together. Did you know Tessa?"

"We went to high school together."

"You were friends?"

"Hardly. Tessa wasn't the easiest person to get along with."

"Oh?"

"She was set in her ways. She couldn't even order a cup of coffee or a bagel without being obnoxious."

"Aren't coffee and bagels pretty straightforward?"

Quincy rolled her eyes. "You would think, right? She wouldn't get coffee unless it came from a cup that had just come out of the package. I like to put the cups out because they look better when they aren't wrapped, and it's faster, and I had to keep a package around just for her, or she would rant about germs."

Marla cringed. "Customer service can be rough. I'm surprised you were so accommodating."

"I wouldn't have been, but my mom insisted. Tessa drank a lot of coffee. She was in two or three times a day and usually had people with her."

"Do you enjoy working here?" I asked. "It's a cute place."

"It's fine. I like talking to people, this job lets me do that." She shrugged. "I need to get back to the counter. It was nice to meet you."

"You too."

She went behind the counter and typed something into the register.

"I didn't realize she worked here," Marla said. "She comes into the hotel at least twice a month looking for Chase. He gave instructions that no one on the staff is to get him for her. Same with McKenzie Taylor. He doesn't want to talk to either one of them."

Quincy looked over at me a few times while we were there. She looked troubled. Now I would have to wonder why.

Chapter 11

The next morning, I woke up to Samson barking. I went into the front room to find him running in circles and jumping on the couch on his way around.

"Samson!" I called.

He ran over and jumped up on me, wagging his tail.

I rubbed his head. "Are you too full of energy? We need to fence all around the cottage so you can be out more. I'm trying to convince Chase to let you into the hotel. What do you think about that?"

He barked once.

"You are such a good boy."

I opened the door and let him out. He would stay near the cottage and come when I called. He was a well-trained dog, but I didn't want to let him out for too long without supervision.

While he was occupied, I got ready for the day and even curled my hair. Not that I was trying to get Chase's attention, but—who was I kidding? I wanted Chase's attention.

By the time Chase stopped in front of the cottage, I felt confident. He stopped and wrestled with Samson for a minute, and I was glad Troy wasn't around to see me watching with a silly grin on my face. He wore cargo shorts and a button-up shirt. I wondered how he could wrestle like that and not lose his flip-flops.

"You ready?" Chase asked.

"Yes." I opened the cottage door. "Inside, boy."

Samson went reluctantly inside, and I closed the door.

"He's getting restless," I said. "He was all over the furniture this morning."

"That's probably my fault," Chase said, opening the passenger's door. That was an improvement. He didn't just hop in and ignore me.

"Why is that?" I asked, climbing in.

"I used to take him running on the beach in the mornings. I haven't been since my aunt left. I should start again." He shut the door, got in his side, and started the engine.

"You run on the beach? Isn't that hard?"

"You get used to it." He pulled out of the narrow driveway and drove around the hotel and onto the road. "Samson loves it. The seagulls don't love him, but he likes to scare them."

"Do you swim?" I couldn't help but glance at his shapely calves as I waited for his answer; he certainly wasn't lying about the beach running.

"You have to swim if you grow up here. I don't even remember learning how."

"I've never been in the ocean."

Chase glanced over at me. "How is that even possible?"

I shrugged. "This is the only time I've lived near it. I keep planning to go down there, but a lot's been going on."

"What do you do back home for fun?"

I wrinkled my nose, not wanting to admit how boring I was. "I like to read and watch movies."

"That sounds *thrilling*."

I smiled. "I'm kind of boring. I'll have you know I've solved several mysteries from the comfort of my sofa."

He laughed. "So you read and watch mysteries?"

"Yep. Mysteries and romance. If it has both, you better believe I'm there."

We drove for a long time in silence. I couldn't think of anything interesting to say. I tried to think through all the clues about Tessa's murder, but there weren't many, and being this close to Chase made it hard to concentrate.

My eyes kept wandering over to him. It might have been best to leave him with his scraggly beard. Now that I could see his lips, it was really hard not to slip into silly daydreams.

"What are you thinking?" he asked.

My head jerked forward, and I tried to remember how long I'd been staring at him. I hoped it hadn't been long, but I had no idea.

"I was just thinking I might have given up on hair cutting too soon. I did a good job on yours."

He ran a hand over his head. "It feels nice. I only need a small squirt of shampoo now. I can't believe I've been wasting so much time in the morning by having that hair. Now I can take a shower and I'm done."

I nodded, glad he seemed to believe my lame excuse for staring at him.

"What did you do before you moved here?" he asked.

"My dad owns a company. I helped wherever I was needed."

"Did you live with your parents?"

"No. I had an apartment."

"And you just walked away from your life when the hotel went up for sale?"

I looked out the window as we got onto the highway. "It wasn't hard. My job was boring, and most of my friends had moved away."

"No boyfriend you left behind?"

My heart began pounding, and I gave a fake laugh. "No. Me and dating don't do well together."

"Oh, yeah?"

"Yeah. I seem to attract... weirdos, which makes me wonder about myself."

He grinned. "It might just be that weirdos are a little more vocal. That's what I've found."

"Maybe. There was this guy who worked for my dad, and he was sure we were meant to be. He'd been bugging me for two years and couldn't get it through his head that it wasn't going to happen. I was thrilled to leave him behind."

"You should bring him here and set him up with McKenzie or Quincy. That would solve both our problems."

I laughed. "Are they that bad?"

"It's been almost twenty years since they first started bothering me. Twenty years. They're both attractive and outgoing. I keep hoping they'll find someone and settle down, but they don't."

"When Tessa died, was her coffee from Betsy's Bagels?"

All humor left Chase's face. "Yeah, it was."

"Could it have been Quincy?"

"I don't know. Tessa bought the coffee, took it home, had some friends over, had a fight with me, then drank it and died. It could have been any of the friends."

"Why did you argue with her?"

"Honestly, I'd been after my aunt to kick her out for a while. She was always causing problems with Sherman and annoying guests who stayed in the rooms to the sides of her. I never would have let her live there in the first place, but my aunt made that call. She was blasting music, and

Sherman was lecturing me on doing my job and keeping the peace. I went over and told her that her guests needed to leave."

He paused and gripped the steering wheel tighter. "I was always calm when I dealt with her, but she was wearing on me. She told me her guests were none of my business. I lost it and yelled at her. I told her she was obnoxious and that she needed to find a new place to live. I don't remember it all, but that's the last time I saw her."

"I hope you don't feel guilty. It wasn't your fault."

"I know, but it's a bad last memory to have of someone. I was one of the last people she talked to. I feel like a jerk every time I think about it."

"I'm sorry." My hand twitched, wanting to reach out and comfort him.

Chase shrugged and exited the highway and drove into the city. He kept looking in his mirror as we drove past the busy stores. His mouth turned down, and he made a few weird turns.

"Is something wrong?"

"Nah. There was a car following us all the way here. I didn't think much about it because there isn't anywhere else to go on that road, but then they followed us on a few weird turns. They seem to be gone now."

We pulled into a hardware store and parked.

"Do you think whoever ruined the chicken coop was connected to the murder?"

"I don't know."

"If they were, it wasn't Sherman. He couldn't have jumped the fence like that."

"Hopefully it was just a prank."

I climbed out of the car and sighed. I hated the smell of home improvement stores, but I would go inside to spend more time with Chase.

⚜

"There's no way this is a coincidence," Chase said, glancing in the rearview mirror. We'd bought things to fix room 202, and I'd gotten enough groceries to last a few weeks, and now we were on our way back home.

"What?" I asked.

"The car's behind us again."

"And you don't recognize it?"

"No. I'm not a car watcher, though. I'm not sure I would know which car belonged to anyone in town."

"Should I call Troy?" I ran my hands over my thighs. We had to do something.

"Yeah. Tell him we should be in town in thirty minutes and to watch for a white Mazda."

I took my phone from my purse and dialed Troy.

"Sheriff McGregor," he said.

"Hi, this is Harmony."

"What's up?"

"Chase and I are driving back to town from the city, and a car's been following us. It tailed us on our way out as well."

"Can you see the plates?"

I looked behind us. "It's too far back."

"What does it look like?"

"It's a white Mazda. We should be in town in thirty minutes."

"Okay. I'll wait for you and see who it is. Don't stop. Come straight here."

I hung up. "He said he'll be waiting and not to stop."

"I'm not really worried, but it's definitely strange."

We drove in silence, and I kept turning to look behind us. The car was keeping a fair distance back.

When we drove into town, we passed Troy's patrol car, and the car behind us turned in a different direction. My phone rang, and I grabbed it.

"Hello?"

"Hey, Harmony," said Troy. "Can you put me on speakerphone?"

I pushed the speaker button. "Alright."

"The car behind you was McKenzie Taylor. What do you think, Chase? Do you want me to go ask her what she was doing?"

Chase groaned. "I don't know. If you talk to her, she'll just argue with you, and it won't make a difference. I should have guessed it was her. It's not like it's the first time."

"That's what I'm thinking. I'm coming to the hotel."

"Stop at Harmony's place. We need to unload groceries."

Troy met us almost as soon as we were out of the truck. They both helped me carry things in and put them away.

"This is a lot of food," Troy said as Samson ran around his legs.

"I don't want to run out for a while." I grabbed the frozen food and put it away first.

"So, what do we do about McKenzie?" Troy asked.

Chase put the milk in the fridge. "I'm guessing we ignore her like usual. I don't get her purpose. What good does following me do?"

"Who knows? She used to do it in high school."

"I wonder if she's been doing it all along and I'm just not observant of those kinds of things."

"It's possible."

"Why doesn't she bother you anymore?" Chase mumbled.

"Because I threatened her with the restraining order, you didn't. Maybe you should."

"I don't want to deal with the problems that would come with that. I'm going to start working on the walls."

"Okay, but I want you to tell me if she follows you again. Once, I'll let it slide, but if she does it again, we need to deal with it." He grinned, and his serious tone dropped to one of teasing. "Or now that we know you have lips, you could start letting people see you in town kissing someone. You might be able to bribe Harmony to do it. Then McKenzie would see she was wasting her time."

Chase punched him playfully on the shoulder. "Don't say stuff like that. You'll give Harmony nightmares."

I glared at Troy but didn't say anything.

"I'm going to get to work," Chase said, turning and walking out the door. He poked his head back in. "Come on, Troy. Hey, Harm? If anything seems weird, call me. Night or day. Alright?"

I just nodded. I'd had several people try to shorten my name to Harm over the years and I'd always protested strongly. But... when Chase said it, my stomach fluttered.

I shut the door behind them and turned to Samson. "What should we make for our employees? Any ideas?"

Samson wagged his tail and followed me to the kitchen.

"I'm thinking something chocolaty and gooey."

Samson sat on his dog bed in the corner. He knew he wasn't allowed to run around the kitchen getting dog hair all over the place.

I washed my hands and sanitized the counter without really thinking about it. My mind was still on Chase. I had to solve this for him, if nothing else.

It had been a long time since I'd made no-bake cookies. They'd give me a little trouble, so I avoided them most of the time. It was time to try them again. I was mainly bad at making them the right consistency. They either turned out crumbly or they never hardened and I ended up eating them off a spoon.

I grabbed the butter and placed it in a pan. I wouldn't ever get better if I didn't practice. Even if I ended up with a pan full of chocolate oatmeal, I was sure most of the staff would appreciate it.

"Cross your paws, Samson. We want to impress people, not make them wonder about us."

Chapter 12

The next week flew by, and I found myself too busy to try to solve anything. I was probably spending too much time trying to make all the staff like me. None of them seemed to dislike me, but I wanted us all to have a good relationship and found that food was the key to happy employees.

This morning, I made cinnamon rolls after Samson and I took a thirty-minute walk in the rain. The smell of cinnamon was a happy addition to the place. They turned out perfectly, and I smiled as I drizzled frosting on top.

Harvey was going to be my best friend. He appreciated my cooking more than anyone else at the hotel.

I covered the rolls and ran over to the hotel. The rain was coming down with a vengeance, so the hotel was full of disappointed vacationers. I'd overheard someone say that

Sherman was visiting his nephew, so I volunteered to help Samantha clean some of the rooms so I could look around without him there.

When we were in Sherman's room, I made sure I was as thorough as I could be, and I tried to look for a remote without tipping off Samantha. I didn't think she would tell anyone, but I needed to be careful.

"It's pretty clean in here," I observed.

Samantha dusted the top of a frame. "Sherman is the cleanest of anyone here. He's picky, though. If you miss dusting for one day, I swear he knows. I don't get a lot of complaints about my work, but you can almost bet that if I do, it's him. He's never left a tip, not once."

"Do other people who live here tip?"

"Chase Jensen does his own cleaning, and Harvey Vaughn tips one hundred dollars a month."

Samantha went into the bathroom, and I peeked in his nightstand drawers. Nothing suspicious.

"Tips at the hotel are good. I'm not complaining," she said from the bathroom. "I just think he could show a little appreciation."

I searched all around the room. I opened the top drawer that was under the TV and frowned. It was full of remotes, charging cables, and cords. Any of the remotes could be what I was looking for, but there was no way to know.

Sherman's nephew had definitely looked guilty when I'd talked to him, but if he was behind it, he wouldn't be able to use a remote since he didn't live here. Maybe things only happened when he visited. Or maybe he had absolutely nothing to do with it.

Thunder boomed in the distance, and I jumped.

"I hate storms," Samantha muttered as she wiped down a surface.

The lights flickered and then went out.

"No, no," Samantha whined. "I don't do dark."

I couldn't believe how dark it was, considering it was still day.

"Do we have a generator?" I asked.

"Yeah, but it's always broken. Mr. Jensen can usually get it going, but it takes a while."

"Well, there's no use staying in here. Let's go to the front."

I opened the door and was surprised to see light in the hallway.

"The hall always has light. I'm not sure why," Samantha said.

Doors kept opening, and people would stick their heads out to see what was going on. We hurried to the front desk and saw Chase rushing down the hall.

"I'll have it on in five," he said as he passed.

"I can't believe how good he looks now," Samantha said.

My mouth turned down. I hadn't meant to make him more attractive to other people. I hoped I wouldn't regret it.

"He's a cutie," Marla agreed. "We sure lose power a lot. You can count on it every time the wind blows."

I put *buy a new generator* on my mental list. I bet that wouldn't be cheap. The list of things this place needed was extensive, and I wasn't sure how to prioritize.

Harvey Vaughn came into the lobby and drew me away from my worries. He was wearing his Sherlock Holmes hat again.

"Hi, Harvey, honey," Marla said. "What can I do for you?"

"Just looking for clues."

"Oh? What type?"

"Any. The lights are out in my room, and I had to take the stairs, so any clues better be on this floor, because I'm not ready to haul myself back up those stairs." He turned and walked around the lobby.

The area was filling up fast. No one wanted to stay in their dark rooms.

"The restaurants around town have power," Marla announced to the room. "And we should have it back on in a few minutes."

A bunch of people went out into the storm. It was probably getting close to dinner.

"Dinner time," I muttered. I had forgotten to make dinner and wouldn't have anything to bring Chase. "I need to go," I said. "Call me if there's a problem."

I pulled my jacket hood over my head and ran through the rain to my cottage. There wasn't any light coming from inside. I always left one light on.

I frowned as I rummaged for my keys. The cottage didn't have a generator; I would have noticed. I unlocked the door and went in.

"Samson?" I called. He'd been a lot more mellow since Chase started running with him again. I whistled. "Hey, Samson!" I shut the door and ignored the thunder and lightning. Something moved to my right. "Samson?" I squinted and tried to see. All I could make out were shadows. It must have been my imagination.

Samson barked from somewhere in the house. I pulled off my jacket and tossed it toward the couch, then twisted to find the dog.

Arms grabbed me from behind.

I screamed as they curled around me, and I stomped on the person's foot and tried to pull away, but they had a good grip. The strong scent of cooked cabbage filled my nose, and I wanted to gag.

"Let go!" I commanded, struggling against him—I was pretty sure it was a man. I tried to elbow him, but he was too close to make a big impact.

"Let the past die," he whispered close to my ear.

A chill ran down my spine. His hot breath was foul against my clammy skin.

A loud crash came from the other room, and Samson came barreling around the corner.

The man pushed me to the floor and ran. I could barely make him out.

Samson tore out the door after him.

I jumped to my feet and chased after Samson. Whoever it was had their back to me, and they were wearing a hoodie.

Samson jumped up, biting the person on the arm. He yelled, and Samson came running back to me. Every few steps, he would turn and bark.

The man soon disappeared around the corner of the hotel.

"Good boy," I said, rubbing Samson's wet head. I led him back into the cottage and called Troy and told him what happened.

"I'll send officers to patrol the area," he said. "I want you to go back to the hotel and stay there until I make sure your house is safe. Take Samson with you."

"Okay. I'll leave the door unlocked."

"Can I search everywhere?"

"Yes."

I hurried back to the hotel with Samson's leash in my hand. The lobby was empty now, so either everyone had gone out to eat or the power was back on.

Chase was at the front desk, leaning over Marla's computer. He frowned when he saw Samson.

"What's going on?"

"A man was in my cottage. Samson bit him." I could still feel his arms around me and shook off the sensation.

Chase came over and rubbed his hand over the dog. "Good boy. How did they get in?"

"I don't know. The door was locked when I got there."

He kneeled and gently pulled open the dog's mouth and looked at his teeth. "I don't see any blood. What was he doing?"

"I'm not sure. He grabbed me from behind."

"He grabbed you?"

"Yeah, but Samson came running, and that scared the man, and Samson chased him and bit him."

Chase crossed his arms. "You can't stay there. This is two times someone's been there."

"I live there. I can't just leave." I sighed. "Sorry about dinner. I didn't get to make anything."

He raked a hand over his hair. "I don't care about dinner. You need to stay at the hotel until this guy is found. Did you call Troy?"

"Yes. He's sending some officers out and checking the cottage."

"I'll call and get pizza, you go sit over there," he said, pointing to a chair in the lobby.

"Why do I need to stay over here?"

He pulled out his phone. "Please?"

I shrugged and went to the chair. I took off my jacket, hung it over a chair near the fire, and then sat down. "Sit," I told Samson.

He obeyed.

Marla came down the hall. "Thanks for watching the desk," she told Chase.

He nodded and walked to the corner.

"Hey, Harmony," Marla said. "Were you out in this mess?"

I touched my hair. It was dry because of my hood, but still messy. "Yeah. It's crazy out there."

"This must be Samson," Marla said.

"Haven't you met him?"

"No. We have a strict no dogs allowed rule in the hotel."

I nodded. "I had to bring him. Someone was in my cottage."

She let out a little gasp. "Oh dearie. That's not good."

"The police are on it."

Chase came over and put his phone on the table near my chair. "The pizza will be a few minutes. The shop is just around the corner. Marla, can you get Harmony a room?"

"Sure, let me see what we've got."

"I'll stay in 202."

"You can't stay there," Chase said. "It's still a mess, and it smells because I just filled the cracks with joint compound today."

"That doesn't bother me. And I still hope to figure something out by being in there."

"Good luck. We tore that place apart."

I didn't need luck. I wouldn't let this mystery slip through my fingers. The carpet had just been one thread, and soon, I'd unravel it all. I had to. "Did Troy ever get someone to check for prints on the clocks?"

"There weren't any. It's not surprising. Someone went through a lot of effort to get that room the way it was. I still can't believe no one noticed when it happened. They couldn't have done it quietly, cutting into the walls and floors the way they did. Troy talked to Sherman, and he doesn't remember anything out of the ordinary from that time period."

"If it were Sherman, he would only have to worry about Harvey and the temporary people to the sides of the room."

"I don't think it was Sherman," Chase said. "It would have taken a lot of work."

"What about Zack? Sherman could have gotten his nephew to do it." Our first encounter still bothered me.

"It's possible."

"He looked nervous when I mentioned something was going on in that room."

We waited for fifteen minutes, and the pizza came.

"Let's go up to the room," I said, grabbing my jacket. "We shouldn't have the dog in rooms people are going to use."

Chase blew out a breath but nodded. "Alright," he conceded, "but pizza might not taste as good with the smell in there."

Chapter 13

We got in the elevator with Samson. The elevator started moving up, and then the lights went out, and we stopped.

"Great," Chase muttered. "Stuck in an elevator with a wet dog."

"Does this happen a lot?" I asked.

"Occasionally."

The light came back on, but the elevator didn't move. Chase handed me the pizza box and pushed some buttons. Nothing happened.

"Why isn't it working? The lights are on."

"Elevators have emergency lights, so they work during power outages."

I sat on the floor, and Samson curled up near me.

Chase pushed the emergency button, but again, nothing happened.

"I left my phone in the lobby," Chase said. "Can you call Marla and tell her we're stuck? Actually, skip her and call Troy."

I reached for my phone, but it wasn't in my pocket. "My phone's gone. I swear I had it." My forehead wrinkled. What was with today?

"Great." He sat next to me and pulled open the pizza box. "At least we have food. I'm sure the elevator will start up soon."

I grabbed a slice of pizza and took a bite.

Chase took a piece and ripped off the crust and threw it to Samson. He looked at it and ignored it.

I ate two pieces, then pulled out a piece of gum. I offered one to Chase, and he took it. I didn't want to be stuck in an elevator with Chase Jensen and pizza breath.

I reached into my jacket pocket to find some lip balm. "Oh my heck," I said, pulling out my phone. "I can't believe I didn't realize my phone was in my jacket. I never put it in there, so I didn't think about it. Sorry."

"No problem," he said as I handed him my phone, and he dialed a number. "Hey, Troy. Harmony and I are stuck in the elevator. Uh-huh... Yep... We have light... What's more important? How can everyone be busy? What about the fire department? Right. So what are we supposed to do?" Chase looked at me and frowned. "Not funny, Troy.

Samson's in here, and it smells awful. Okay, fine, but try to hurry. Bye."

"They're busy?" I asked.

"Yeah. I guess they still have some officers looking for the guy from your cottage, and lightning struck a building, so the fire department is on that. He said there's a ton of crazy stuff going on and they might not be around until morning."

"Morning?" I squeaked. "I can't stay in here until morning!"

"I'm not sure there's a lot of choice. I'm guessing the elevator will start before that."

All I could think about was the fact that the elevator didn't have a bathroom. I was okay now, but by morning, it was going to be bad. And how long would Samson last?

I leaned against the back wall of the elevator and sighed. "This could be a long night. Did Troy have any suggestions?"

"Yeah, but you don't want to hear what he said."

"Could Harvey help? He used to be a cop."

"He's not so good at fixing things. He tried to fix his microwave once and ended up shocking himself pretty badly."

We sat for what felt like forever. I thought about scrolling through my phone, but that would waste the battery that we might need later. It also wouldn't feel fair to Chase, who didn't have a phone.

Samson eventually ate the pizza crust, then curled up on the floor once more.

"I guess we should try to sleep," Chase said. "It will make time go by faster."

I nodded. It was early, but I might be able to sleep. "At least the floor is carpeted." I rubbed my hand over the green carpet. "Not very padded, though." I tried to decide what would be better. Wearing my jacket, or wadding it up and using it for a pillow. It was the first time it had been cold since I'd moved here.

"It's rare to get storms like this. We get a lot of rain, but we rarely get thunder and lightning."

Chase scooted into the corner and leaned his head against the wall. It looked like he was going to sleep sitting up.

I curled up on the floor and faced away from him. I tried to use my arm as a pillow, but I could already tell it was going to be a terrible night.

After trying to get comfortable for ten minutes, I sat up and pulled off my jacket. I folded it up and put it under my head.

This was impossible. Now I was cold. I wrapped my arms around myself and shivered. I sat back up again, pulled my jacket back on, and lay down.

Chase chuckled softly. "Maybe we should get padded carpet for the elevator in case something like this ever happens again."

I sighed. "I'm never going to sleep. Samson makes it look so easy." I looked at the dog. He was in a deep sleep.

"Samson and I have that in common. We can sleep anywhere and through anything."

"If it wasn't cold, it would be alright... Well, if it wasn't cold, and I had a fluffy pillow. I think I'm a picky sleeper."

Chase smiled. "I've never heard of a picky sleeper before."

"My dad used to tease me. He said I could only survive if the temperature was seventy point two degrees. I can't sleep if I'm hot or cold, so I was always in control of the thermostat."

Chase's smile slipped away, and his eyes narrowed as he looked at me.

"What is it?" I asked.

"I'm trying to decide how much of a gentleman is left in me."

I laughed. "What do you mean?"

"I could give you my jacket so you could sleep better, or I could be selfish and keep it."

"I won't take your jacket."

"If Samson wasn't wet and smelly, I would say you could cuddle up by him."

"It'll be fine. One bad night isn't the end of the world."

Chase scooted over next to me.

My heart began pounding as I wondered what he could be doing.

He laid on his back and stared up at the ceiling. "This carpet really is bad." He took off his jacket and put it under his head.

I wrinkled my nose. "It's old too. All the carpet here is."

He nodded. "There's no way that isn't awkward to say this. Come over here and lie on my shoulder. Then you don't have to lie flat, and it will be warmer."

I blinked and stared at him.

"I swear I'm not trying to make a move. It just makes sense."

I felt like I was frozen to the floor. There was nothing I would like more than to cuddle with Chase Jensen, but that didn't make me feel less awkward.

He rolled his eyes. "I know, I'm the scary guy, but you aren't going to get any sleep otherwise."

My mouth turned down, and I sat up and scooted closer. "You aren't scary," I said, resting my head against his shoulder.

He put his arm around my back, and I resisted cuddling in close. I didn't sleep on my back, so this wasn't going to be much more conducive to a good night's sleep. It would be better if I turned to my side, but then he might feel my crazy heartbeat—and it would give away my secret.

At the top of the elevator, I saw a small blinking red light. I tilted my head and squinted to try to see it better. There was a small one-inch ledge at the top going all the way around the elevator. Whatever blinked was sitting on the ledge.

I sat up and pointed. "Do you see that light?"

Chase looked up. "Interesting." He stood, reached up, and grabbed something. He turned and showed it to me. It was a small rectangular thing with buttons.

"What is it?"

He smiled. "A remote. And it looks homemade."

My eyes went wide. "To the clocks?"

"That's my guess. It has a lot of buttons. I'm going to put it back, so it only has my fingerprints on one spot."

"This means it could be anyone. I was thinking it had to be someone who lived here, but not if someone was doing it from the elevator. Maybe someone pushes the buttons every time they get in the elevator. Are there cameras in here?"

"No. Cathy always had a reason to not put any up. In reality, she didn't like spending money on the hotel. There are cameras outside and in the lobby, but that's all."

"Great. Now I'm going to be thinking about this all night. It's just another thing that will keep me from sleeping."

"Well, I'm tired and plan on sleeping," Chase said, putting the remote back where we found it.

He lay back down, so I went back to his shoulder and tried to ignore how uncomfortable it was. If I could turn toward him, it would be better, but then it would seem natural to put my arm around him, and I didn't want him to think I wanted to cuddle with him, even though I did.

"You seem stiff," he said.

"I'm not a back sleeper," I admitted.

"You can turn. Just drape your arm over me. It will be warmer."

It was like he'd read my mind, but it still felt odd. I wasn't used to feeling awkward. I prided myself on going through life without feeling embarrassed about things that couldn't be changed, but maybe that was only because I'd never been thoroughly tested.

I turned and put my arm across his stomach.

I wished it were dark because my face felt hot, and I didn't want him to know how much turmoil grew inside me. I angled my face down so he wouldn't notice. My face grew even warmer when I thought that if I just looked up, it wouldn't take much to kiss him.

I really needed to get control of my thoughts. I hadn't even known the man for an entire month, for goodness' sake.

It felt like hours before I could relax and began to drift to sleep. The last thing I remembered thinking was that I hoped I didn't drool on Chase's shoulder.

I heard sounds that I couldn't place, but I didn't want to open my eyes. I felt so tired and warm. A voice made me pry them open, though.

I was disoriented for a moment, and then I remembered. I still had my arm around Chase, but something was different. Samson was lying on my legs. I looked at the elevator door and saw Troy smiling at us.

I sat up quickly and ran a hand over my hair. Chase sat up and yawned, and Samson jumped up, barked, and ran into the hall.

"Is it morning?" Chase asked.

"Yep," Troy said, holding out his hand. Chase grabbed it as Troy pulled him up.

"Show him the remote," I said as Chase helped me up next.

"Remote?" Troy asked.

"Up there," I said, pointing. "We think it's the remote for the clocks."

"I put it back, but it has my prints on it," Chase said.

"Let me run and get some gloves from my car."

I held in a yawn. "I'm going to room 202," I said. "I'm going to stay there until I make my cottage more secure."

"Good idea," Troy said.

"Come up when you're done," Chase told Troy. "I'm going to go and make sure there isn't anything dangerous for Samson to chew on or anything."

I wanted to protest, but I was too tired. I'd wanted to sleep a little longer before starting the day.

Chase found Samson and led him to the room.

I frowned when we got in. The smell wasn't strong, but it was messy. All the construction things were lying around. Staying here might've been a bad idea. Chase was still going to need to paint it, and I would be in the way, and there were too many things for Samson to get hurt on.

Samson ran in and jumped onto the broken bed.

"I guess I'll need to get a different room," I said. "I don't want to be in your way while you're working. Were you planning on working in here today?"

"I was," Chase said, "but now I'm tired, I doubt I'll get to it until tomorrow."

"Good, then I'm going to take a nap," I said, falling back onto the bed.

"Won't that be nice for you?" Chase said, grinning slightly.

"Take today off," I said. "Go sleep. Nothing will fall apart if you rest one day."

"If I sleep all day, then I'll be awake all night, and the cycle will never end."

I could hear Troy talking to someone in the hall.

"I'm going to talk to Troy for a minute," Chase said. He went into the hall.

I sighed. I didn't want to move, but I wanted to know Troy's opinion on the remote. It wasn't easy pulling myself off the bed, but I walked over to the door. It hadn't latched all the way, and I paused when I heard Troy.

"You look like trash, man. Did you sleep at all last night?"

"A little," Chase said.

"I thought you could sleep anywhere. I've seen you sleep in some weird places."

"You try to sleep when you have Harmony Landing cuddled up next to you. Actually, I'd rather you didn't."

I smiled. Did that mean Chase might like me?

Troy chuckled quietly. "So, you've hit the cuddling stage already? That's not like you."

"Don't be an idiot. It was cold last night."

"Alright, don't get defensive, just because you had a bad night."

"I didn't say it was a bad night. I just couldn't sleep."

"Did you kiss her?"

"What? No!"

"Did you want to?"

"What do you think?" His typical sarcastic twang made me smile even more.

"You should have."

"And scared her away? I hardly know her."

"She's changing you. I can see it. You never say more than a word or two to anyone except me, but you have been since she came."

"I don't want to talk about this."

I took small, quiet steps back. I didn't want to be caught listening at the door. The conversation they were having wasn't one I was sure I could handle.

Sinking back onto the bed, I grimaced. The bed smelled funny. It was probably covered in all sorts of construction dust. Samson jumped up on the bed and put his head on my stomach. Now it smelled even worse.

Chase came back in. "Are you sure you want to stay in here?"

"No. It's dirty and it stinks. Not as bad as Samson, though."

"I'll call and schedule him a bath. There's a woman who does dog grooming from her home. I bribe Troy to take Samson every once in a while. She even gives him a bowtie that I'm pretty sure embarrasses him to death. He tries to chew it off as soon as he gets home."

Samson barked.

Chase laughed. "See? He knows what I'm talking about."

"Did your aunt get Samson as a puppy?"

"Kinda, I had a friend who gave him to us when he was a puppy. I was so happy to get a dog, but Cathy was pretty bossy about everything. I guess it worked out because he's well-trained. He always liked me the best, though, didn't you, boy?"

Samson just stared at him, and I patted his head.

"I think he has a new favorite," I said with a mischievous smile.

"You might be right. Samson has good taste."

Chapter 14

Two days went by, and I'd been staying at the hotel. Chase had painted room 202, and tomorrow someone was coming to install new carpet. The once-perceived *haunted* room was going to be the nicest in the hotel.

Since Samson was staying with me in one of the rooms, we were going to have to have someone deep clean the carpets in case we had a guest who had a dog allergy.

Troy texted me and said he wanted to meet in the lobby, so I hurried down. He was sitting on a chair near the fireplace. There wasn't a fire today, because it was warm again.

"Hello," I said, sitting across from him.

"Hi," he said and placed his soda on the side table. "I never told you what I found in your cottage."

I felt my stomach fall. "You found something?"

"Whoever it was came in the back door. They broke the lock. Chase fixed it yesterday, so you'll need to get the key from him."

"I've never gone out that door, so it's not important."

"There was also a note on your table. It said something along the lines of leaving things alone."

I felt a chill run down my spine. "Great. I've been staying here because Chase is insistent, but I wasn't worried until now."

"Chase is going to put cameras on your back fence and on the front of the cottage. He's actually working on it right now."

"Did you find anyone?"

"No. Keep a watch on people's arms. If Samson bit them, they might have a mark. I don't think he bit them hard because Chase said there wasn't any blood on Samson, so it might not come to anything. I already looked at Sherman's arm, and it looks normal."

"It couldn't have been Sherman," I agreed. "He wouldn't have been able to jump the fence, and I doubt he could have held onto me the way the man did."

"We have to consider it might not be the same person who smashed the chicken coop. It probably is, but I don't want to overlook anything."

I nodded. "When Tessa first died, did you check out Betsy's Bagels?"

"Yes. I have some surveillance of Quincy handing Tessa the cup. There's nothing weird about it. She grabs a cup, fills it, and hands it over."

"So, it had to have been poisoned later."

"That's my theory."

"Do you still have the video footage?"

"Yeah."

"Can I watch it?"

He grinned. "If it makes you happy."

"I know I'm weird, but I feel like I'm missing something."

"We're all missing something, or this case would have been solved. Do you want to walk down to the station, and I'll show it to you?"

"Sure."

We got up and strode out into the warm sun.

Chase was outside fixing a sprinkler. "Where are you two headed?" he asked.

"My office," Troy said.

"Why?"

Troy grinned. "Why not?"

"He's going to show me a video from the day Tessa died."

"I'm coming," Chase said, tossing a piece of PVC pipe on the grass.

"Like that?" Troy asked, pointing at Chase's dirty hands.

"Yep."

We walked to the end of the block and turned, passing another hotel, and headed toward the ocean. The police station was on the road that looked out at the beach.

"It's too bad our hotel isn't on this street," I said. "It would be nice to be right on the beach."

"There's one hotel that is," Chase said. "It's about a block over. It's falling apart worse than Harmony's, so we still get good customers. Almost everything on this street is a gift or hobby shop or a restaurant."

The police station was a small red brick building with only one level. Troy let us in and led us past the front desk that was surrounded by bulletproof glass.

A woman manned the desk and barely looked up as we passed. We entered an office, and Troy sat at the desk.

"Sit," he said. "Let me pull it up." He began typing on the computer as Chase and I sat in the two chairs in front of the desk.

"This office is small," I said.

Troy nodded. "This county has three police stations. Most of the towns are small and can't support one. I rotate between offices but spend most of my time in this one." He turned his monitor around and pushed a button. "Here we go."

Footage from Betsey's Bagels came up. The video was black and white. It showed Quincy and another woman

I didn't know handing people food. After a minute, a woman in a fancy skirt and blazer came in.

"There she is," Chase muttered.

"That's Tessa?" I asked.

"Yes."

Tessa walked up to the counter. I wished I could hear what everyone was saying. The angle of the camera was looking at the counter, so I couldn't see Tessa's face. Quincy didn't look thrilled to see the woman. She bent down and grabbed a foam cup and then swiveled to fill it with something.

"See?" Troy said. "She did the same thing she did for everyone else. I've zoomed in on the coffee dispenser and her hands, and nothing weird is happening."

"Can we watch it again?" I asked.

"Sure," he said, starting it over.

I sighed as I watched. There wasn't anything here. Not that it surprised me. The person who had attacked me was strong, and I was almost sure I could take Quincy in a fight.

"We had the remote checked for prints. There weren't any. Well, except Chase's, and we already knew he touched it."

I frowned. "If someone made it, wouldn't it be hard not to leave prints?"

"They could have made it with gloves on, or cleaned it well."

"But if they use it in the elevator, they would always have to wear gloves as well."

"It's not hard to keep a glove in a pocket."

"I guess."

"I need to get back to the sprinklers," Chase said. "Are you going back?" he asked me.

"I think I might go back to Betsy's."

Troy stood. "I'll come with you."

Chase scowled. "Don't you have work to do?"

Troy grinned. "I figure escorting Harmony to the shop is part of my job. Someone needs to make sure she's safe after the break-ins at her place."

Chase shook his head but didn't say anything.

We went back out and walked back to the hotel. Chase returned to the sprinkler, and Troy and I walked down the street to Betsy's Bagels.

We entered the shop and ordered some bagels. I wasn't going to get one unless someone besides Quincy was at the counter. Luckily, she wasn't there. Even though she looked innocent, I wasn't going to test it by eating anything she handled.

We sat at one of the small tables, and I scanned the shop. Nothing stood out any more than the last time we were here.

"Maybe I should be paying attention to McKenzie," I said. "She was following us, after all. That seems suspicious."

Troy ripped off a piece of his bagel. "McKenzie goes through little phases. She's trailed Chase before, but it's been years since she last did it. At least that I know of. I was a little surprised when she did it again last week.

"I've only met her once."

"That's probably plenty."

"Troy?" Quincy said, coming out of the back room. She flashed a one-hundred-watt smile and approached our table with a newfound bounce in her step. "You haven't been in for years!" she said, sitting at the table with us.

Troy frowned. "Bagels aren't my thing."

"Everyone likes bagels," she said, resting her arms on the table and leaning toward him.

Troy leaned back against his chair and looked like he'd be happy to run.

"We should catch up sometime," she said. "Do you want to meet at Francisco's later this week? They have a new pasta dish that's great."

"I don't think so," he rebuffed her.

"Why not?"

"Because I don't want to. We've been down this road before."

Quincy frowned. "I thought you'd changed. I guess not."

Troy raised his eyebrow. "I'm in here with a woman, and you just asked me out. You haven't changed either."

Her eyes narrowed, and she looked at me. "You're with her?"

"I'm here with her."

"But are you dating?"

I couldn't believe how forward this woman was.

"Nah. I don't think Chase would appreciate that."

Quincy pressed her lips together. "Chase? Chase is dating her?"

I thought about telling her she could ask me herself, but I already had a feeling a fight was about to break out. Troy was letting old problems resurface here. He was trying to make Quincy mad. I'd never seen him like this.

Quincy glared at me. "Chase doesn't date anyone. Chase doesn't *talk* to anyone."

"Things change," Troy said.

"Then why are you out with Chase's girlfriend? I know you guys are close, but you can't share everything."

"I'm not Chase's girlfriend," I said.

Troy grinned for the first time since we came in. "But we all know it's going to happen."

"Do you know what? You should stay out of my shop," Quincy said. "Both of you. And tell Chase I don't want him in here either."

I raised my eyebrow.

Troy nodded, grabbed his bagel, and tossed it in the trash. "It's no good anyway, and Chase hasn't been here since high school. Come on, Harmony."

I tossed my bagel and followed him out the door, but I struggled to keep up with Troy's long strides. "Troy, slow down," I said.

"Sorry," he said, slowing. "Quincy makes me so mad. I thought I'd gotten over the harsher feelings I had for her, but I guess I haven't. I just stayed away from her until I blocked her memories out or something."

"Did you feel the same about McKenzie and Tessa?"

"No. They bugged me, but not to the same degree. Sorry about dragging you into it. Now Quincy's probably going to spread it around town that you're dating Chase. Honestly, I think the two of you are a good idea."

"We hardly know each other."

"Yeah, but I have a gift for seeing these things." His mischievous smile came back as some of his tension dissipated. "If I didn't get elected sheriff, I could have become a matchmaker."

I laughed. "I'll keep that in mind if I ever need a match."

He grinned. "I already placed you with Chase. Believe me. It's perfect. No one else in the world would have been able to get him to cut his hair. I know, I've tried. His aunt Cathy begged him to cut it. Some guys can pull off long hair and beards, but Chase isn't one of them."

We made our way back to the hotel and stopped and watched Chase cover up the hole he'd made.

"I need to get going," Troy said and turned to me. "You forgive me, right?"

I smiled. "There's nothing to forgive."

"Later, Harmony. See ya, Chase."

Chase nodded and wiped his brow. Troy hurried off, and I stared after him.

"What was that all about?" Chase asked.

I shrugged. "Troy and Quincy had a bit of a fight at Betsy's."

Chase took a deep breath. "He shouldn't have gone there. I could have predicted that would happen. That's why he was apologizing?"

"Well, he also told Quincy you were dating me. I think he was saying everything he could think of to make her mad."

Chase rolled his eyes. "Great. Something like that will spread like wildfire." He sighed. "Poor Troy."

I raised my brow. "How so?"

"Troy had a huge crush on a girl in high school. Neeley was her name. He never dated her. She was one of our friends. The three of us were always together. She wasn't like all the other girls trying to get our attention. No one knew he liked her except me.

"A few years after we graduated, he finally asked her out. She said yes, but then Quincy told her that Troy only asked her because he wanted to be able to say he'd dated every girl in his graduating class. She broke off the date, and Troy's never forgiven Quincy."

"What happened to the girl?"

"She's from the town next to us. I haven't seen her in years. As far as I know, she's still there."

"Does Troy still like her?"

"No, but it still makes him mad to think about." Chase stomped on the dirt to pack it down. "And now we have to convince the town we aren't dating. It might ruin any prospects you have."

I laughed. "Prospects? Never heard someone say that in real life. I'm not looking for a relationship, so I'm not bothered by it." I knew I was lying, but it slipped out. Chase was the only person here who had caught my eye, and I didn't want him to think I was out looking. Of course, now he might think I wasn't interested in him either.

"I'm going to go to my cottage to make dinner," I said.

Chase frowned. "I don't think you should be there."

"It's daytime."

"It was during the day the last time someone broke in."

"But it was stormy and dark. Besides, they probably just wanted to leave the note, but then I came in. I doubt they'll be back."

"I'm coming with you."

"Will you go get Samson first? He hasn't been outside much today."

"Sure. I'll meet you there."

I watched him leave and frowned, wondering what the chances were of getting stuck in the elevator with him again.

Chapter 15

C hase started meeting me every day at five o'clock and sitting at my table while I made dinner. It didn't make sense to carry food back to the hotel, so he stayed and ate, and then did the dishes.

If we were trying to get people to think we weren't dating, this probably wasn't the best way.

I spread melted butter over my rolls and put them on a platter to cool. I'd started staying in room 202 now that it was painted and had carpet, but all I really did there was sleep. It didn't have the musty smell that the other rooms had, so now I was more determined to remodel the others. No one wanted to stay at a smelly hotel.

Chase was keeping Samson outside with him as much as possible while he worked on the grounds, too. I'd noticed Chase never said a lot unless I brought things up first.

I hadn't figured out anything new about Tessa, and I was beginning to wonder if I ever would. Maybe Troy was right. It had been so long that there might not be any clues.

"Do you like oatmeal cookies?" I asked as I checked on the potatoes.

"So long as they don't have raisins," he said.

"I think I'll make some for the staff."

"Did you still want to turn that nook at the hotel into a breakfast shop?" he asked.

"I do, but I've been so busy I haven't looked into it."

"If you trust me, I can get the process moving."

"I trust you, but you do so many things around here. I don't want you to burn out or anything."

"Working helps me stay sane. I've always done better when I'm busy."

"Troy said you were on the football team. I bet that kept you busy."

He nodded. "We were on every team. Well, not every team, but a lot of them. That's what happens when you have a small school. Almost every guy in school was on the football team. We didn't even have tryouts. We had to beg some people who didn't like sports to come just so we didn't have to forfeit."

"If you want to work on the breakfast nook, that would be great. I'm still trying to decide what to serve."

"Start out small. You don't want to make too much work for yourself."

"If things go well, I'll hire help."

"It's going to go well. None of the hotels have restaurants, so I bet we would get more business if we were the only ones to have a breakfast option. It might be better to raise the price of a room and offer free breakfast."

"I'll have to think about that."

"Just make sure it's not too healthy, but that there is a healthy option. You'll always get someone like Sherman. He's into healthy eating, and if you don't have a healthy option, he'll give you a lecture on the benefits of cooked cabbage."

I laughed. "Sherman is an interesting guy." I dumped my potatoes into a bowl and began mashing them.

"Let me do that," Chase offered.

"Thanks." I stepped aside.

He took over the mashing, and I flipped the steaks.

My mind whirled. "Does Sherman eat a lot of cabbage...?"

"He used to. The smell made people complain, so we had to tell him he couldn't cook it in his room. Now he goes and eats it once a week with some of his relatives. Don't ever let him get started on the benefits of cabbage and improving digestion. He'll never stop talking, and by the time he's done, you'll be convinced you need cabbage. Then you eat it and realize it still tastes like cabbage."

"The man who attacked me smelled like cooked cabbage."

Chase looked up at me. "Are you sure?"

"Positive."

"Maybe it was Sherman."

"No. The guy moved too fast and was thinner. Maybe his nephew. I really thought that Zack seemed nervous when we were talking about room 202. Next time he comes, we should see if he has a bite mark on his arm. How often does he come?"

"I'm not sure. I see him about once a month, but I'm not usually around people if I can help it."

"I keep thinking it might be him."

"Just because his uncle eats cabbage doesn't mean that he does."

"I know, but that's all I've got right now."

"Have you always been this way?" he asked, going back to mashing the potatoes.

"What way?"

"Trying to solve mysteries."

"Pretty much. I actually solved two crimes back in my hometown. They weren't anything big, but it makes me wonder if I missed out on what I should have done with my life."

I glared at the price tag on the bag of chocolate chips. It was the only ingredient I needed that I didn't have. They cost three times the amount of anywhere else I'd ever shopped.

I'd been secretly hoping to see McKenzie when I came in, but the one person at the register appeared to be sixteen.

I grabbed two bags of chocolate chips and took them up to the register. The cashier scanned them, and I paid. As I was walking out the door, McKenzie walked in.

"Hello, again," she said.

"Hi."

"I'm not sure if I got your name last time?"

"I'm Harmony."

"Right. You're the one dating Chase Jensen." She was smiling, but her eyes were shooting daggers. "You have to watch out for that one, but I suppose you know that."

I was going to tell her we weren't dating until she added the last part. I tilted my head and studied her. "Watch him?" I asked.

"You know, he was questioned about a murder a few years ago."

"Questioned, but not convicted. From what I've heard, there was no evidence pointing to him at all."

"No evidence, but it looked bad."

"Chase is a good guy, and I don't listen to gossip." That was a lie. All I'd done since I came here was listen to gossip.

"I'm not doubting you," she said, running her hand through her blond hair. "Chase and I had something going on in high school. I was a cheerleader."

I smiled. "How nice for you." I didn't know what else to say.

"Cheerleaders and football players were always together."

I nodded. I wasn't sure if that meant anything, since Chase said everyone was on the football team.

"He was on the basketball team as well. I cheered at all his games. You can go see the yearbooks at the library. They go back for years. I have an entire page dedicated to me."

"I think I know what's wrong with this town."

She narrowed her eyes. "Oh?"

"You're all stuck in the past. You were a cheerleader like, what, seventeen years ago? And it's still something you bring up in the first few minutes of the conversation. Everyone who grew up here has told me about high school. None of you left. You all stayed in this small place and held onto the past. No one gets over anything."

I wasn't sure why I said it. Things just pop out of my mouth before I think them through.

McKenzie rubbed her lips together and glared at me. "I'm not stuck in the past."

"So you would never follow the guy you had a crush on into the city and stalk him?"

Her eyes went wide, then narrowed again. "You don't know me."

"No. I don't. Have a nice day." I clutched my chocolate chips and walked home. I probably hadn't handled the conversation correctly, and if I wasn't careful, I might end up being banned from more than just the bagel shop.

When I returned home, Samson was in the backyard with Chase while he worked on the coop again. I went inside, seized the mixer, and plugged it in.

I should probably tell Chase that the rumor had gotten around that we were dating, but then he might wonder why I hadn't denied it.

I grabbed some butter and put it in the bowl as I replayed my conversation with McKenzie over and over while I mixed the cookies. There were so many things I could have said that would have gone better.

I added extra chocolate chips, because it felt like that kind of day.

Then I put the first batch of cookies in the oven and cleaned while they cooked. When the timer beeped, I pulled them out, and satisfaction filled me. They looked perfect, and they smelled great.

I put in another pan and turned when someone pounded on the door.

Figuring it was best to be cautious, I looked out the window and saw Chase. I opened the door, and Samson ran in.

"I'm done for today, so I was bringing Samson back. It smells really good in here."

"I just made cookies. Come in and I'll give you some. They're too hot to eat right now."

Chase followed me to the kitchen, and I grabbed a paper plate and my spatula. "How many do you want?"

"Not too many. Just like seven or eight."

I looked up to see him grinning at me.

"How many would you want if you wanted a lot?" I scooped eight cookies onto the plate.

"I was joking," he said. "Just give me two."

"Too late," I said, handing him the plate. "You better enjoy them. I've never paid that much for chocolate chips in my life."

"You got them in town?"

"Yes. McKenzie was there." I turned the spatula nervously in my hands.

His jaw tightened. "What happened?"

"She made me mad, and I was rude. Now I'm regretting it. It's probably not good to insult the only grocery store owner in town. I've already been banned from Betsy's Bagels."

He shoved a hot cookie in his mouth. "What did she say?"

"It doesn't matter. I should control myself."

"Was it about me?" he asked with a mouth full of cookie.

I shrugged.

He wiped his lip. "I won't get upset. I've heard it all before."

"Well, for one thing, the rumor has gotten around, she thinks we're dating."

He grinned. "I hope you let her think that."

"I did, but only because I was angry. I pretty much told her it was time to get over high school and move on."

"Ouch. I'm sure she loved that."

"Now I'll never dare go back in there."

"Just stock up on anything you might need next time we go to the city. I never go to her store." Chase always avoided conflict, while I often found myself in the middle of it, so I wasn't sure his advice would do me much good. "These are great cookies. Are you taking some up to the hotel?"

"I will once they're all done."

"You're going to be everyone's favorite person. My aunt never made them cookies."

I smiled. "That's my goal."

There was another knock on the door, and I answered it, and Troy came in.

"It smells awesome in here."

Chase held out his plate, and Troy took one.

"You owe me this," Troy said, grinning at me.

"I do?"

"Yep. Because of you, I just had to talk to McKenzie. She said you came into her store and harassed her. That's why I'm here. I probably deserve two cookies."

"I wasn't harassing her. It's probably your fault when it all comes down to it. She said she heard I was dating Chase."

Troy took another cookie. "Oh, good. I'd hoped that rumor would get around." He almost sounded gleeful.

"Why?" Chase asked. "You need to get some hobbies or something. You have too much time on your hands if you're creating gossip."

"I'm telling you, it will be good for your image. People will stop staring at you and blaming you for everything."

"Not unless you find out who killed Tessa."

"I'm trying."

"I'm going to do it," I said. "I can feel it."

"You should probably leave that up to me and the police," Troy said. "You don't want to put yourself in more danger."

"You've had years."

"But it feels like things might be coming together."

Chase swallowed a bite of cookie. "That's only because of Harmony. If she hadn't started looking into the hauntings, we still wouldn't know about the clocks."

"True. I never thought the room and the death were related. I didn't really even hear about people thinking the room was haunted, except as a joke. I didn't realize people were actually hearing things in there."

"Maybe I'm crazy, but I can't ignore something like that," I said. "Even though we figured out what was going on in the room, the housekeepers are still scared of going in there. Samantha said she'll still scare herself, so she doesn't want to clean it."

"I would be scared going in by myself," Troy said. "Even though I know there's nothing in there, I would psych myself out."

Chase chuckled. "And that's coming from the sheriff."

I grinned at Troy. "You're the first sheriff I've ever met, and it's changed my opinion about what I always thought a sheriff would be like."

"What did you think they would be like?" He cocked his head.

Chase threw a rag at Troy, and he caught it. "Probably more mature."

"Hey, I can be mature if I need to be. It's just good to relax when you can, especially in a high-stress job. I don't want to become grumpy and old before my time." He gave Chase a pointed look.

Chapter 16

"We're really gonna run down the beach?" Marla asked me, patting her bright red ponytail.

I couldn't help smiling when I saw Marla's bright pink shorts and purple tank top. Her shoes were neon blue. She would stand out next to me. I had black yoga pants and a green T-shirt on. We were standing on the road in front of the beach.

"Apparently it's a big thing here. Chase does it, and so does Zack Bradley."

"And that's why we're here. To find Zack Bradley?"

"I talked to Sherman, and he told me Zack runs on the beach every morning before work."

"So we just run around and hope we bump into him? Then we look at his arm to see if he's been bitten by a dog?"

"That's the plan. I bet he starts over here, since this would be the obvious entrance from town. Do your shoes have a heel?" I asked, looking at her blue shoes.

"It's a wedge, and only a small one."

"I doubt that's good to run in."

"Probably not, but I want to look fabulous when I'm running."

"How long do you think you can run?"

"Oh, I'd say about one minute before I need a breather. I might be able to go for two, but I also might pass out."

I smiled. "I bet I can do two. I don't know how we're going to pull this off."

"We don't start running until we see him."

"He does this every day. I doubt we can catch up to him if he's already running. Maybe we should go down to the beach and watch for him. Once we see him, we start running. He'll have to pass us."

"Sounds good to me."

"I might not recognize him. I've only seen him once."

"I'll know him," Marla said. We walked down to the beach, and I wondered how anyone could run on sand. I was having a hard enough time walking in my running shoes.

"He usually comes at this time," I said, looking back at the road.

"Sherman just gave you all this information? Didn't he think it was a little suspicious that you would want to know the time and place his nephew goes running?"

"Sherman likes to talk, and likes to complain. All I had to do was ask what Zack did for fun, and Sherman talked for fifteen minutes without pausing. He also told me he keeps track of points for Zack. Inheritance points."

Marla snorted. "What does that mean?"

"When Zack does things for Sherman, he gets points. If he annoys him, he loses points. Once Sherman dies, Zack will get a certain amount of money, depending on how many points he gets."

"Ahh. I've actually heard Sherman tell Zack things like, 'good job, ten points.' I never knew what he meant."

"It's a little weird."

Marla smiled and pointed at me. "I bet you're thinking that Zack wanted to get on Sherman's good side by keeping people out of the room above him. That would have to be worth a lot of points."

"It has crossed my mind..."

"Look, there he is."

I looked over and saw him walking down from the road. He was wearing red shorts and a white shirt.

"Let's run," I said. We began running through the sand, and I felt like a complete amateur. The sand made me more clumsy than I already was when I ran.

Marla was holding her hands out to the side like she was on a balance beam. At least I didn't look ridiculous by myself. People's eyes would be drawn to her because of her arms.

"How do we know if he's behind us?" Marla asked.

"I don't know. We aren't going fast, so it shouldn't take him long to pass us." I took a clumsy step and my ankle bent funny, and I fell to the sand.

"Are you alright?" Marla asked.

"Yes. I don't think I was meant for running."

Zack came jogging over. "Did you break anything?" he asked.

"It's fine," I said, rolling my ankle in circles. It was throbbing a little, but nothing I couldn't walk off. I brushed the sand from my hands onto my shirt and looked up at Zack. He was wearing long sleeves. "You run in long sleeves? Isn't that hot?"

"I prefer it," he said. "It helps me get warm faster."

"Hey! What's going on?" Chase ran toward us, and Samson took off after some seagulls. Did everyone run at this time?

Zack held out his hand and helped me up.

I cringed when I tried to put weight on my foot. Maybe it was worse than I thought.

"I'm fine," I said. Then my mouth might have dropped slightly at the sight of Chase with no facial hair. He'd shaved!

He'd been attractive before, but now he was gorgeous. The tan he'd worried about was hardly noticeable.

"Take a step," Chase said.

I forced a smile. "Not while you're all watching."

"Can you walk?"

I didn't want to try and fall again. This was embarrassing enough. I put a little pressure on my foot and winced. Before I could protest, Chase scooped me up and began walking up the beach to the road.

"Do you need help?" Zack asked.

"Nope," Chase said as Marla came running up next to us. Chase whistled. "Come, Samson!" The Golden Retriever darted toward us.

"I can walk," I said, not wanting to be paraded across town. That would be uncomfortable.

"Liar," Chase said.

"You don't want to make it worse, hon," Marla added. "Rest and ice are what you need."

I put my arm around Chase's neck so it would feel less weird.

"You shouldn't start out running on sand," he said. "That's a more advanced thing."

"We don't want to run," I said. "We were hoping to run into Zack."

"Well, I guess that worked."

"He had long sleeves, so we couldn't see if he had a dog bite."

"How did you know he would be here?"

"Sherman told us. It sounds like he runs a lot. Do you ever see him?" I asked. The more I talked, the less I would think about his hard muscles beneath my hands.

"No. I don't pay attention to people I pass, so I could have run by him a hundred times and never known."

"You shaved."

"And it looks good," Marla said.

Chase grimaced. "Yeah, after you trimmed it all, I realized how nice it is not to have the upkeep. I thought it might be nice to not have hair in my mouth and keep food out of my beard."

I caught myself right before I almost ran my hand over his cheek. I don't know how I would have explained that.

When we got to the road, I turned to Chase. "I think I can walk. I just needed to rest it for a second."

"Why chance it?"

"I'm gonna run on ahead and get some ice ready," Marla said, taking off at an awkward run. She held her hands the same way she did when she was on the sand.

Chase chuckled. "I've never seen anyone run like that."

"You don't need to carry me two blocks. Your arms are going to be sore."

"It's not a problem."

"Everyone in town is going to see."

"They're gossiping about us anyway."

I gave up and tried not to make eye contact with anyone we passed on the street. After a minute, a car pulled up next to us. I looked up and saw Troy's patrol car.

He rolled down the window. "Do you two need a ride?"

"Yes," Chase said, walking over to the car.

Troy jumped out and opened the passenger door. Chase put me gently down, and I slid into the back. Chase got in on the other side with Samson.

"What happened?" Troy asked as he drove toward the hotel.

"I hurt my ankle," I said. "But I think it's fine."

"I wasn't sure if you were hurt or trying to stir up gossip."

"That's your goal, not ours," Chase said.

Troy laughed. "Well, I'm sure this helped. Is that Marla?" Troy stopped, and we picked her up.

She got in the passenger's seat and tried to catch her breath. "I haven't run in a long time! Now I know why I don't."

"Do lots of people run with long sleeves?" I asked.

"Some," said Chase.

"I bet he was covering a dog bite," Marla said. "How do we figure it out? Can you go ask to see his arm, Sheriff?"

"See whose arm?"

"Zack's."

"I guess I could ask, but it might be a little suspicious."

"But it's to solve a case," I said.

Chase turned to me. "I'm not sure someone's uncle eating cabbage is enough reason to demand to see someone's arm."

"I'm lost," Troy said. "What does cabbage have to do with anything?"

"The man in my cottage smelled like cabbage," I said. "Sherman likes cooked cabbage, but I know it wasn't him."

"I'm with Chase. I don't see how that would point at Zack."

"I know, but how many people really like cabbage?"

"Not me," Troy said.

"It could be a family thing. If Zack is trying to impress his uncle to get more money, then he might make cabbage for him since he isn't allowed to cook it at the hotel."

"I feel like I've missed things, and they don't make sense," said Troy. He pulled up to the front doors of the hotel, and Chase jumped up and ran around to my door.

I got out and put light pressure on my foot. It hurt, but it would probably be barely noticeable by morning.

Chase picked me up again.

"I'm fine," I protested.

"Good," he said. "Let's keep it that way."

Marla had already rushed into the building, probably looking for ice. I ignored all the stares as Chase carried me across the lobby and to the elevator.

On the second floor, we got off, and he took me to room 202.

We entered, and he put me on the bed. It seemed silly since I was just going to get up and walk as soon as he left.

Samson jumped on the bed, and Chase pulled him off. "Now stay," Chase said.

"Me, or Samson?"

"Both."

I raised my brows. "Forever? It's still morning. I'm not going to sit here all day."

He frowned, and Marla came in carrying an ice pack. She kneeled by the bed and began untying my shoe.

"I'm fine, Marla. I can get it."

"Don't make it worse," she said, pulling off my shoe and sock. "Bless your soul, it's gonna bruise."

I looked at my ankle, and my mood soured. "I don't have time for this." It wasn't terrible, but it was slightly swollen, and the bruising was already showing.

"I'll call the doctor," Marla said, as she put the ice pack on my ankle.

"No, I don't need a doctor. It's going to be fine. Does anyone know where Zack lives?"

"No," Chase said. "And I don't think you should go to his house. I'll talk to Troy again and see if he can go check his arm for a bite. I'm going to take Samson to my room and want you to rest."

"We don't always get what we want," I said with a smile.

He scowled.

"I don't see any reason to be in bed all day. I'd die of boredom."

"Marla, call me if she tries to leave the hotel," Chase said.

"And what?" I asked. "You'll come tackle me and drag me back?"

"Yep." He turned and left with Samson.

Marla winked. "He's gone on you like a June bug on a porch light."

I laughed. "What is that supposed to mean?"

"He likes you."

"No, he's just a good guy."

She tilted her head and put her hands on her hips. "I've been around here long enough to know that you've changed that man. He's gone from growling and ignoring people to whistling when he's working on a project. I see the way he looks at you. He's as smitten as a kitten."

I sighed and flopped my head back on the pillow. "I don't know."

"You better stake your claim, hon. Now he's shaved off that thing he called a beard, all the women in town are going to be lined up trying to get his attention."

I covered my head with my hands. "I know. I should have let him keep his crazy facial hair. My dad always had a beard, and it looked decent. That one Chase grew was pretty crazy."

"He never trimmed it. That was his problem. So, what are you going to do about him? You need to act fast."

"I'm not going to do anything. McKenzie and Quincy are both attractive, and Chase didn't like them because of the way they acted. I don't want him to categorize me with them."

"You aren't a thing like them. I've only known them a short time and can already tell they think the sun just comes up to hear them crow. Chase can see that, too. He's a smart man."

"I don't know him well enough to do anything."

"Well, from what I've heard around town, everyone already thinks the two of you are practically engaged," she said.

"That's Troy's fault. When do you have to be at the front desk today?"

"Nine."

I stood and took a step. It hurt, but nothing too bad. "Does that give us time to go find Zack's house and snoop around?"

Marla tilted her head. "Like breaking into his house?"

"No, just look around the outside."

"I bet we could do that."

"I'm not sure how we get his address."

"He lives on my street."

"Oh. That's a weird coincidence."

"Have you been around this town, darlin'? There's not much to it."

"So, do we go?"

"Of course we go."

Chapter 17

This had been a stupid idea. We were in the garage of Zack's little red brick rambler, and my ankle and foot were throbbing. We hadn't taken time to think that Zack would probably come home to shower after his run, and not only that, but he'd come out to the backyard where we'd been looking around.

The back door to the garage had been open, and when we heard his door creak, we'd snuck in. The only way out was to open the big garage door, which would make noise, or go into his house.

If that wasn't bad enough, we had Samson with us, and he was pulling hard against his leash.

"Is he still out there?" Marla asked.

I peeked out the crack in the door. "Yes."

"What's he doing?"

"Just standing there. Who just goes and stands in the backyard?"

"The weather's nice. I would."

I sucked in a breath and pulled away from the door. "He's coming this way!"

The SUV in the garage took up most of the space. I squished between the vehicle and the metal garage door and pulled Samson with me. I tried to ignore the spider webs clinging to the door. My back rubbed against the SUV. Marla was right behind me in her red heels and purple dress.

When we passed it, we hurried to the side and got down by the tires.

"What if he comes over here?" Marla whispered.

"I doubt he can fit past the vehicle. He would have to come through the house." I hoped I was right. There was a door on this side that went into the house, and I was counting on him not being able to slip past his SUV. We'd barely made it, and he was considerably bigger.

My biggest fear now was that Samson would bark.

Zack was whistling when he entered and rummaged through something.

My heart was pounding so hard I was surprised he couldn't hear it from across the garage.

Then I let out a relieved breath when we heard the door slam.

"Well, I just lost about two weeks of my life," Marla said, standing. "I think my heart just about jumped outta my throat."

I turned around and saw a long wooden workbench. It was a mess. A small black plastic rectangle caught my eye. I bent over to look at it, and my eyes lit up.

"This looks just like the remote we found at the hotel," I said, pointing.

Marla's brows came together. "Why would he have more than one? It wouldn't do him any good from here if he's trying to control things at the hotel."

"Troy said the remote was homemade. Maybe Zack just likes to do this kind of thing. Of course, this doesn't prove he made the one at the hotel, but my guess is he did. It looks just the same. I bet you can get them in kits."

"We need to get out of here before he comes in."

I nodded. "You're right." We squeezed back past the vehicle and stood by the door. Now that it was closed, I was nervous to open it a crack to see if he was gone.

"Do you think he's still there?" Marla said quietly.

I shrugged and slowly turned the knob. I peeked out and sighed when I didn't see anyone. "Let's go," I said, hurrying out the door.

We rushed from the garage and around the house and down the street. My foot was tingling, and it was taking everything in me to walk normally. Maybe I had sprained something.

"Are you alright?" Marla asked. "You're limping. Chase is gonna chew me out if I let you hurt yourself more."

"I'll be fine. I should probably stay off it for a while after this." I wouldn't admit that to Chase.

"Let me take Samson," she said, taking his leash.

We ambled the couple of blocks to the hotel, and I made it into the lobby and sank down into a chair. My entire right leg was shaking.

"I'll get ice," Marla said.

"No, I'm fine. I just need to sit for a minute."

"Harmony?"

I turned to see Chase walking toward me.

"I can't stay in my room all day," I said before he could say anything.

"Where were you? I've been looking for you for at least twenty minutes."

"We went for a short walk."

He turned to Marla. "There's something all over the back of your dress."

Marla turned in a circle and tried to see her back.

I grimaced. She must have gotten dirt on her from rubbing against Zack's vehicle. I remembered rubbing against it, so I probably looked the same.

The front doors opened, and Zack walked in. He was wearing slacks and a long-sleeved button-up shirt, and his hair was still wet. He looked around, and when his eyes fell on me, he came over.

I swallowed hard and tried not to look guilty.

"Hello," he said, looking from me to Marla.

"Come to visit Sherman?" Marla asked with an enormous fake smile. I hoped I didn't look as shamefaced as she did. Samson sat by the chair and panted.

"No, I thought you two might be looking for me. I saw you leaving my backyard from my window."

Chase crossed his arms and fixed me with a stare. I couldn't think of any reason to have been in Zack's backyard.

"It was my fault," Marla said. "I was holding Samson's toy and swinging my arms too much. I let go, and it sailed into your yard. Samson ran after it, so we followed him."

Chase shook his head.

"Oh, okay," Zack said. "I just wanted to make sure you didn't need anything. Excuse me. I should check on Sherman since I'm here, hope you all have a nice day."

"You too, hon," Marla said with the same fake smile.

Zack walked off and around the corner to the elevator, and Marla let out a long breath and sat on the armrest of my chair. "Goodness gracious, I almost perished."

"Why?" Chase asked. "What were you two up to? Why were you walking?" He looked at me, and I rubbed my lips together.

Marla waved her hand through the air. "We snuck into Zack's garage. Not on purpose, just because we needed to hide. We weren't really doing anything. We found a remote, though, so it was worth it."

Chase blinked twice. "You two are going to get into trouble." He didn't appear pleased but couldn't hold back his curiosity. "What kind of remote?"

"It looked like the one we found in the elevator," I said.

"Hmm. I'll tell Troy."

"Why don't you help Harmony back to her room?" Marla said. "That adventure wasn't good for her ankle. I didn't think she would make it back. She was going as slow as molasses in January."

"Marla!" I hissed. I didn't want Chase hauling me back upstairs. Hotel rooms were boring, and I wasn't one to sit around watching television all day. "I'm fine. I'm just going to stay down here and people watch for a while."

Chase bent down and started taking off my shoe.

I pulled my foot away.

"Let me look at it," he said. "Then we can decide whether you need to go to the doctor."

"*We* can decide? I hate to tell you this, Chase, but you're not my dad."

He raised his eyebrow and grabbed my leg. "And I'm glad about that." He pointed down at my ankle. "Look at this. It looks a lot worse than it did earlier. You shouldn't have gone walking on it. You need to take your shoe off so it doesn't get swollen and hard to get off." He untied it and gently slipped it off my foot.

I tried not to cringe at the pain.

"I'll call the doctor," Marla said.

"No. Let me wait a few days and see what happens."

Chase grabbed another chair and pulled it in front of me. He lifted my leg and rested it on the chair. "How's that? Do you need a pillow?"

"It's good."

"Do you want me to leave Samson here so you don't get bored?"

"Sure."

"I'll take him to get some water and be right back." Chase hurried off with Samson.

I glared at Marla. "Why did you tell him everything?"

"He asked. You don't wanna start lying to the people who care about you."

Zack came walking back with his hands in his pockets. "Sherman's sleeping. I'll see you all later."

Marla waved. "Bye."

"Hey, Zack?" I called. "I'm sorry I stomped on your foot the other day."

"No problem," he said, then immediately frowned as the color left his face. "I don't even remember it happening."

"Ha!" Marla said. "Too late! You can't backpedal now."

He scratched his head. "I don't know what you're talking about."

We were already past the awkward, so we might as well continue. "Will you show me your arm?" I asked.

"My arm?"

"Roll up the sleeve," I said.

His eyes narrowed. "That's a really weird request."

Chase and Samson came back, and Samson growled at Zack.

Zack's eyes went wide, and he took a step back.

"Samson, stop," Chase said. The dog darted toward Zack, growling, and Chase grabbed his collar and pulled him back. "Samson! Knock it off. I don't know what's gotten into him."

Zack didn't take his eyes off the dog. "Dogs aren't supposed to be in here."

"Just like you weren't supposed to be in my house?" I asked. I realized I might be jumping to conclusions, but I was almost sure I was right.

"What are you talking about?" Zack said. "I wasn't in your house."

"Then show us your arm."

"I don't want to show you my arm."

"Why?"

"Why do you want to see it?" he challenged.

Marla rolled her eyes. "To see the dog bite."

"You guys are all crazy." He spun around and hurried out the door.

Samson growled but stayed with Chase.

"You just demanded he show you his arm?" Chase asked.

"I told him I was sorry for stomping on his foot, and he said it was okay, then tried to say he didn't remember it ever happening."

Troy came into the lobby, pushing Zack in front of him. His gaze fell on us. "I've been looking for you," he told Zack. "Why were you running?"

Zack pulled away from him. "Because that dog is crazy," he said.

"Guess what just came back from the city?" Troy said. "I sent some of the clocks in to get them tested better for fingerprints. My guy in town isn't always the most thorough. They found one small fingerprint on one clock. Wanna guess whose it was?"

Zack clenched his jaw and scowled.

"Yep, yours."

"What clock?"

"One that was stuffed in a wall in room 202."

"That doesn't make sense. I don't go in there."

"But you did when you placed them there, didn't you?"

"And Samson doesn't seem to like you," Chase said. "Maybe because you broke into Harmony's place?"

"I don't have to talk to any of you," he said.

"No, you don't," Troy said. "But how hard do you want to make this on yourself?"

"What's going on?" Sherman asked, coming over.

"Should we be doing this right here?" I asked. I was a little worried about how it would affect business.

"Everyone, to the event room," Troy said.

I frowned. "The event room?" I watched everyone walk over to a door a few feet from the desk. I stood and followed slowly behind.

Upon entering through the door, I gasped in shock as my mouth opened wide. The room was huge! It had blue carpeted floors, a stage, and nothing else.

"Where did this room come from?" I asked when I went in.

"It's always been here," Marla said. "People rent it out."

"I thought it was a closet or something."

"What's going on?" Sherman repeated.

"Someone has been messing with the room above you for years," Troy said. "Trying to make it look haunted. Zack's prints were on something that no one could touch by accident."

"Anything can be an accident," Sherman said.

Troy arched his eyebrow. "I don't think you can accidentally touch something that has been hidden in a wall. And why would he do that? He has nothing to gain."

"You complain more than everyone else in the hotel combined," Marla said. "Maybe he didn't want to listen to you complain about upstairs neighbors anymore."

Sherman turned to Zack. "Did you mess with the room?"

"I don't have to say anything without an attorney."

"Zack?" Sherman said, a warning tone in his voice.

Zack ground his teeth and glowered at his uncle. "I haven't done anything that wasn't to protect you."

"Protect me? How?"

"I'm not going to say it. You know what."

Sherman pushed his glasses higher up his nose. "I don't have to be protected from anything."

"I was just trying to keep you from going to prison," Zack said. He turned to Troy. "None of it was malicious. No one was hurt by anything I did."

"Why would I go to prison?" Sherman asked.

"For murdering Tessa."

Chapter 18

"I did not kill Tessa!" Sherman said. "How could you ever think something like that?"

Zack took a deep breath through his nose. "Right now, we both need to stop talking and get really good attorneys."

Sherman crossed his arms. "I don't need an attorney. I didn't do anything. You, on the other hand—"

"Everything I did was to protect you!"

"And what did you do?" Troy asked.

Zack glared at Troy. "I'm not talking to you."

Samson was baring his teeth and not taking his eyes off Zack.

I tapped my lip. "You think Sherman killed Tessa, so you rigged her room up to scare people away. It would also be in your interest to have that room remain empty because then Sherman would have the quiet he wants."

"I do deserve quiet," Sherman said. "But Zack, it's not your job to do something like that."

Zack ran his hands through his hair and gripped it. "Not my job? Your comfort is my job, as you so frequently remind me. I can't be around you without worrying about your comfort every second. If the wind blows in the direction you don't like, I lose inheritance points for not blocking it for you adequately. No one can be sane and live like this!"

Sherman scowled. "I'm not *that* difficult."

Marla's brows rose. "Oh, you are that difficult, darlin'. Everyone here knows it."

Sherman's lip turned down, resembling a pouting toddler. "I just know what I like, and I'm not afraid of letting people know it."

"Sherman's a millionaire," Chase said. "If he wanted to, he could rent out the room above him to have quiet."

Sherman's eyes widened. "I never thought of that."

"So you killed Tessa." Zack shook his head.

"I didn't."

"You did. I'm tired of covering for you. I don't care if I lose my inheritance. You're burning me out."

"Of course you lose your inheritance! I can't believe you damaged the reputation of this hotel. They lost businesses from not being able to rent out that room."

Zack's teeth cracked. "You were glad no one stayed there."

"Yes, I was. But you had no right."

"And you had no right to kill someone. My crime is much less than yours."

Sherman poked Zack in the chest with his pointer finger. "I bet you killed her and now you want to blame it on me because you know they're close to figuring it out."

Zack turned to Troy. "The night Tessa died, Sherman was spitting nails angry. She'd been partying for three nights in a row, he was sick of it. He would normally send me up to tell her to be quiet or have me complain to the office. He said I wasn't getting results, and he was going to deal with Tessa once and for all. If that doesn't sound guilty, I don't know what does."

Sherman's face was red with rage. "How dare you accuse me? All I did was go upstairs and have a talk with her. I told her I was going to call the cops every time she disturbed me until she straightened up."

"What did she say?" I asked.

"She said, 'I'll be happy to deal with Troy every day. Send him on over.'"

Troy grumbled something to himself.

Sherman wiped his brow. "I was going to give her another piece of my mind, but Miss Taylor came for a visit, so I left, and—"

Troy looked up sharply. "McKenzie Taylor?"

"Yes."

Troy's fists clenched. "Why didn't anyone ever tell me McKenzie was there? I questioned everyone in the hotel, no one ever mentioned her."

"I'm sure I did when it happened," Sherman said.

"No," Troy said, scrunching his eyes. "In fact, you never even told me you'd talked to Tessa that night. I have detailed notes and I've been reviewing them."

"There wasn't much of a reason to bring up our little talk. It didn't have anything to do with the murder."

Troy took a deep breath. "You don't get to decide that. When I asked you where you were that night, you should have mentioned talking with her."

"I knew if I did, I would become a suspect, and then I would have to deal with more boring questions."

"I'm not going to be in trouble for messing with the room, am I?" Zack asked. "I did it to help someone, after all."

Chase snorted. "To help someone cover a murder."

Troy fixed his eyes on Zack. "I guess it depends on whether Harmony presses charges. It caused thousands of dollars' worth of damage."

"I'll pay for all the repairs," he said.

Troy ran a hand over his face. "I need to think. Don't leave town, either of you," he said, looking from Zack to Sherman.

Zack nodded and hurried away.

Sherman began walking leisurely to the door. "I didn't mean to withhold anything. I figured it didn't matter since I was innocent."

"It would have been nice to know McKenzie had been there," Troy said.

Sherman waved over his shoulder and was gone.

"Now what?" Marla asked. "Should we go talk to McKenzie?"

"Probably," I said.

"Whoa, whoa," Chase said. "When did Troy deputize the two of you?"

"I'll handle this," Troy said.

Marla and I shared a look.

"I guess I should be at the front desk," Marla said.

I didn't have anywhere I had to be, but resting was probably a good idea. I was having trouble thinking past my throbbing ankle.

I sat on an empty chair up at the front desk with Marla and Anna. At least I think her name was Anna. She was quiet, and I'd only talked to her once.

Troy grabbed a pen from the desk and a pad of sticky notes and began writing things as fast as he could.

"Afraid you're going to forget something?" Marla asked.

"Yep. I learned early on to write everything as soon as possible. Even things I think I could never forget get forgotten if I'm not careful."

"Are you taking Chase with you?" I asked.

Chase shook his head. "I'm not a cop. Troy has officers who work with him."

I nodded and looked out the clear sliding doors. McKenzie, Quincy, and a man were walking toward the hotel. They weren't together, just going in the same direction.

McKenzie and Quincy kept shooting glares at each other.

Something about the man made my stomach drop.

When he got closer, I cringed as I recognized Rex Parker. There was no way he was here by coincidence. He was here for me—to beg me to move back home and date him. I never would have believed he would follow me here. I'd told him I wasn't interested more times than I could count.

"You alright, honey?" Marla asked. "You just went pale."

I dropped onto the floor behind the desk. "Tell that man I'm not here."

Chase and Troy both grinned down at me. Marla looked confused, and Anna shrank like she wished she weren't there.

"Who is he?" Troy asked.

"A guy from back home. I do *not* want to talk to him. If he asks, tell him anything to get him to go away."

Troy chuckled. "That bad?"

"Welcome to Harmony Landing," Marla said.

"Hello," I heard Rex say. "I'm looking for Harmony Landing. The person, not the hotel."

"She's not here," Marla said. "You can leave a note."

"Hi, Troy. Hello, Chase," McKenzie said.

"I can give Harmony a message," Chase said, ignoring McKenzie's greeting.

"Who are you?" Rex asked.

"He's Harmony's boyfriend," Marla said.

I wanted to slap my forehead. I'd expected that from Troy, but not Marla. I had said to tell him anything, so I couldn't blame her.

"Her boyfriend?" Rex asked.

"Yep," Chase confirmed. "What do you want me to tell her?"

"How can she have a boyfriend? She hasn't been here that long."

"Sometimes people just connect," Marla said.

"Well, I guess I'll just get a room."

I sighed. I'd hoped he would take off.

"Alrighty," Marla said, typing something into her computer. "How long do you want to stay?"

"I'm not sure. At least a week."

There was no way I was going to be able to avoid him for a week.

"Is everyone going to ignore me?" McKenzie asked.

"Nope," Troy said. "You're going to have more attention than even you know what to do with in a minute."

"What are you talking about? Why are we even here?"

"I was wondering that."

"Harvey Vaughn came by my store and said I needed to come to the hotel," McKenzie told them.

"I just came to talk to Chase," said Quincy.

"There's Harvey now," Troy said. "I wonder what he's up to."

I wished I weren't hiding behind the desk. I wanted to see what was going on.

"Harvey, why did you send me here?" McKenzie asked.

Harvey laughed. "I thought it was better to get everyone together to see how it all goes down."

"All what?" Troy asked.

"Everything about the murder. I've been listening around and feel pretty sure you're about to solve everything."

"Why bring me?" McKenzie asked.

"I figured they might be ready to blame you."

"For a murder?" McKenzie squealed.

"Can I just get a room?" Rex asked. "Or I can come back later?"

"Good idea. Go get lunch and come back," Marla said. I really wanted to pop up, but I couldn't see a way to do it without looking crazy.

"Why would you blame me for a murder?" McKenzie asked, high-pitched. "I haven't even heard of a murder."

"Tessa," Troy said.

"You think I killed Tessa? Why would I do that?"

"Well, you did fail to mention that you spoke with her the night she died," Troy said.

"It wasn't important. Nothing worth mentioning."

"What did you talk about?" Troy asked.

"It was years ago. How am I supposed to remember? It wasn't anything out of the ordinary, whatever it was."

"The fact you didn't come forward and tell me is concerning."

"Why? I didn't have anything helpful to say."

"Why does everyone think that makes it their call? When I asked everyone in town who had talked to her that day, that included you. You don't get to make your own rules."

"I was only there for a minute. I think I was returning something to her."

"You still should have come forward."

"Sherman was there," McKenzie said. "When I got there, he was there."

"I know, and that's something you should have shared with me five years ago, too."

"Do you suspect Sherman?"

"He has always been shady," Quincy said. "But I would guess it was McKenzie over Sherman."

"Why are you even here?" McKenzie demanded. "I know you come here to try get a glimpse of Chase, but don't you think you should grow up and move on?"

"I'm not the one who follows him every chance I get," Quincy said.

I really wished I could see everyone's expressions. I could only see Marla and Chase's backs. Anna had gotten up and gone somewhere.

"I don't follow him."

"Everyone in town sees you. I've seen you follow Troy as well. I wouldn't be shocked if you killed Tessa," said Quincy.

McKenzie let out a low growl. "Why would I do that?"

"Because you owed her money, maybe?"

"It was hardly anything. Nothing to kill someone over. Besides, tons of people owed her money."

"Why did I not know this?" Troy asked. "There should have been records if people owed her."

"That's why I was there," McKenzie said. "I was paying some of it back."

"How much?"

"About twelve thousand."

Troy whistled. "Did you pay in cash?"

"I don't remember."

"How could you not remember? There was no money in her room when I searched it. I can have her accounts checked to see if anything was deposited."

"I didn't do it!" McKenzie squealed. She sounded like she was on the verge of a breakdown. "Tessa was acting weird. She kept putting her hand to her head and muttering things. I admit it. I thought she was drunk, so I told her I gave her the money, but I kept it and left."

"After poisoning her," Quincy said.

"No! Why aren't we looking at Sherman? He was there before me, and she was acting like something was wrong when I got there."

I wanted to believe it was McKenzie over Sherman. Neither one of them was my favorite people, but she bothered me more. It seemed strange that both of them had withheld information. I understood not wanting to look guilty, but not telling made them both look suspicious.

A new thought formed in my mind, but it wasn't making enough sense to vocalize yet. Still, that had never stopped me before. I didn't always create a comprehensive theory before spitting things out.

"This doesn't look good, McKenzie," Troy said.

I stood up, hoping no one would notice that I hadn't been there all along. McKenzie and Quincy both frowned at me, so I guessed I failed.

"It sounds bad," I said. "But it wasn't McKenzie. It was Quincy."

Chapter 19

Quincy's eyes went wide, and everyone stared at me. I wasn't completely sure, and I might've ended up completely embarrassed, but there was only one way to find out.

"I didn't kill Tessa," she said.

"No?" I asked. "You know Troy has a video of the day Tessa got her coffee at your shop."

Quincy shrugged. "So? I gave him the video. It's not something I don't know."

"Have you ever seen the video?"

"Sure. I saw it when I gave it to him."

"And you still gave it to him?"

Quincy swallowed. I'd made her nervous, even though I was bluffing. There was no way to prove the suspicion that had entered my mind, so I needed her to confess.

"Why wouldn't I?"

"Because of what they might find."

Her eyes narrowed. "There wasn't anything to find."

"Tessa would only drink out of cups that were still in the package. You put the poison in the cup, then put the cup back in the package. You didn't do it in the shop. Those cups were only for Tessa, so you could grab the cup, fill it with coffee, and no one would be the wiser. Even if they watched the surveillance."

Quincy's eye twitched. "I would never."

"You made the mistake of holding the cup at an angle that the camera could see inside," I lied. "There was something in the cup before you filled it."

"That doesn't mean I did it," she said, taking a step back. "Anyone at the shop could have put it there."

"But you should have seen it inside when you went to fill the cup, and even if you didn't know what it was, you should have gotten a new cup. It was you."

"Whatever. I'm leaving." She swung her hair over one shoulder as she turned and began walking to the door.

Harvey stepped in front of her, blocking the way.

She twisted back to us. "You don't believe it was me, do you, Troy?"

Troy frowned and didn't say anything.

"Everyone knows Tessa was a jerk. Why should anyone care who killed her?"

"That's not helping you," Troy said. "Did you owe Tessa money?"

"Why would that matter?"

"Did you?"

"A little."

"How much?"

"I can't remember. Just because I owed her money and don't care that she's dead doesn't mean I did it."

The sound of glass breaking reached our ears, and we all turned to peer down the hallway. It looked like one of the housekeepers had crashed their cart into the wall.

"She's running!" McKenzie yelled.

Quincy had taken off, past Harvey and out the front doors.

Troy rolled his eyes and charged after her. Harvey was close behind him.

"That was unexpected," McKenzie said. We all stared at her. She cleared her throat and looked around awkwardly.

"Do you think Troy needs help?" I asked.

"Nah," Chase said. "Troy is good at what he does, and Harvey's still sharp. They'll deal with it."

"I'm gonna go find Anna and tell her it's safe to come back," said Marla. She walked out of sight.

I frowned when I saw Rex coming back up the sidewalk.

Chase put his arm over my shoulder and turned to McKenzie.

"McKenzie? I'm getting a camera and putting it on the back of my truck."

She scowled. "Why are you telling me?"

"You know why."

Her lips drew together as she crossed her arms, and she stomped out of the hotel just as Rex came in.

I tried to escape, but Chase still had his arm over me.

"Hi, Harmony," Rex said, raking a hand through his dark blond curls.

"Hey."

"What have you been up to?"

I held in an eye roll. "Just running my hotel. Why are you here, Rex?"

"It was time for a vacation, so I thought I might as well come see you."

I shook my head. I'd never led him on in any way. I'd been so blunt it felt mean, but he didn't seem to get it.

"I know you said you weren't ready for a relationship, but it looks like you changed your mind," he said, motioning to Chase. "You know I would have come if you'd said you were ready now."

"Rex, I told you. You aren't my type."

He frowned. "And this guy is? You barely know him. You've known me for years."

"Yes, and that means I know without a doubt that I don't want to be with you."

He scratched his cheek. "I'm going to stay around a while. Just to let you decide for sure."

"I already decided."

"Well, I'm going to try change your mind."

I frowned.

Marla came back, and Rex went up to her and began registering for a room. Chase still had his arm over me and led me out of the hotel.

When we got outside, we saw Troy putting Quincy into the back of his patrol car. Harvey was standing nearby with his hands on his hips.

"If Quincy is guilty, people here should stop blaming you for things," I said.

"Maybe."

"Now what? You become an extrovert again?"

He chuckled. "I'm not sure I've got that in me anymore, but I guess it's possible. I can't believe I didn't see anything in the coffee cup when we watched the video."

"There wasn't anything," I admitted. "I figured all the evidence was gone, so I went on a hunch. I could have been totally wrong."

He laughed. "That was brave."

"Or just stupid. It worked, though."

"Tell me about this Rex?"

I sighed. "You saw him. He's always like that. I told you... only weird guys like me."

"So… unless we want to make Troy a liar, we have to pretend to date until Rex leaves."

I frowned. "Is that okay? That goes way beyond your job description."

"Yeah. Troy's my best friend. I can't have him looking like a liar, but I'm not sure you can handle me pretending to be your boyfriend."

I peered up at him. "What are you talking about?"

He grinned as he watched Troy drive away. "I might do such a good job that you actually fall for me."

I grinned and shook my head. "You wish."

Zack came out of the hotel. I hadn't realized he was still inside. He avoided looking at us as he left through the parking lot.

"Hey, Zack!" I called.

He turned and appeared tired. We walked over with Harvey at our side.

"You never showed us your arm," I added.

He scowled. "Stop with the arm thing."

"I will once you show us."

"Why do you want to see his arm?" Harvey asked.

"Because someone broke into my house, and Samson bit them on their right arm. I think it was Zack."

Harvey grabbed Zack and pulled up his sleeve while Zack struggled. I was impressed that Harvey could manage it. He was twice as old as Zack.

Zack yanked his arm away and took a few steps back, pulling down his sleeve before I could get a good look.

"I might have overlooked the fact that you messed with the hotel, but not that you broke into my house."

He took a deep breath. "I didn't hurt anyone. You're the one who should be charged for letting your dog attack people."

"It's actually a positive thing to have a dog that will attack intruders," Chase said. "And Samson is my dog, so if you want to complain on your way to prison, you can complain about me."

Zack glared at us as he climbed into his SUV and slammed the door.

"I'll tell Troy," Harvey said. "I need to go on a walk anyway, and by the time I get there, he'll probably have Quincy locked up."

"I'm going to move back into my cottage," I said as we watched Harvey leave, too.

Chase frowned. "Not until Zack is no longer a threat. I think you should get a fence to go around the property."

"I was thinking that might be good. Then Samson can be outside as much as he wants. I could get a dog door, but I'm not sure he could fit through one."

"You would be surprised at what that dog can fit himself through."

"What did you mean, Samson is your dog?" I teased. "I'm pretty sure he lives with me."

He grinned. "I feed and clean up after him. If you start doing that, I'll gladly let you say he's yours."

"Maybe we can have joint custody."

He laughed. "Sure."

Chapter 20

The sun was beginning to set and made a pretty pink and purple pattern against the sky. I sat on a sun lounger at the beach with Marla the next evening.

Marla was engrossed in her book. It wasn't easy for me to get into a book while outside. I'd never spent time on the beach, so I kept getting distracted by the sounds and people.

Marla said the beach was a place for contemplation and reflecting on life. I might get there, but it wasn't going to happen until it stopped feeling so interesting—so new.

I'd had Chase take me to the store today so I could get a beach outfit. I wasn't exactly sure what a beach outfit was, so I went with a picture I'd seen once. I got a yellow sundress and matching sandals, and a floppy hat to top it off. I'd had to take off the hat because I couldn't lean back with it on.

I pushed my sunglasses up onto the top of my head and put my book down when Samson came running over to me. He sat and placed his chin on my stomach, tail wishing in the sand.

"Hello, buddy. Are you having fun?"

He looked up at me.

"Are you with Chase?" I hoped he was. If not, it meant he had escaped the cottage, and I was sure I'd locked it.

I turned around and saw Chase and Troy. They didn't look like they were ready to hang out at the beach. Troy was still in his sheriff's uniform, and Chase was wearing a polo shirt and jeans.

Samson ran up to meet them as I stood up. My feet immediately disappeared into the sand, and I frowned. My sandals weren't beach-friendly. The bruise on my foot and ankle looked terrible, but it felt a lot better today.

"So, this is where people hang out," Troy said. "You two are hard to find."

"I'm converting Harmony to beach life. If we're lost, we're here," Marla said, barely looking up from her book.

"Quincy confessed," Troy said. "She went on a long rant about what an ogre Tessa was and how she deserved it all. I didn't realize Tessa loaned so many people money. I knew the family was rich, but I didn't know she had access to the money. Quincy borrowed thousands of dollars from her, even though the two of them didn't get along. She didn't have the money to pay her back, and Tessa was threatening her."

"Wow," I said, petting Samson when he came up to me. "What happened to Tessa's family?"

"They moved just after she died."

"And what about Zack?"

"He's in custody," Troy said. "He also admitted to everything he did. Even to trapping you in the room. He ruined the chicken coop to take your focus off the room, too. It sounds like he was trying to scare you off. At least he seems mostly repentant. He's also embarrassed that he jumped to a conclusion and caused a problem. I don't think Quincy has the decency to feel guilty."

Chase nodded. "That sounds about right. She's always been self-centered."

"You did a great job, Harmony," Marla said. "You solved a five-year-old case."

I shrugged. "I don't feel like I really solved it. In the end, there was no evidence, and I made a crazy guess that just happened to be right."

"But you were right, so you have good instincts."

"And you figured out why everyone thought room 202 was haunted," Chase said. He smiled, looking proud. "It's not going to change anything, though."

I tilted my head. "What do you mean?"

"I saw Samantha walking past the room holding her breath this morning. She's still scared."

"Great. So we still can't rent it out?"

"Probably not. Or we could charge more so people could have an experience. Lots of weirdos like things like that. Or I can take the room and you can rent out mine."

"We can do that if you want," I said. "You made it a lot nicer than all the other rooms, so you deserve it."

"It sure smells better than the other rooms."

"And I bet you're quiet enough you won't bug Sherman. Is Sherman staying?"

"Yes. He said getting accused of murder isn't enough to interrupt his routine."

Troy laughed. "Good for him."

"I was kinda hoping he'd leave," Marla said. "Every time I see him walking toward me, I have to force a fake smile on my face. And now, without Zack, I'll have to deal with him more."

"Maybe we should tell him he isn't allowed to complain so much," I said. "Like give him a monthly allowance of complaints."

Chase grinned. "He wouldn't be able to stick to it. I like Sherman. If you don't take him seriously, he grows on you. And he can play a mean game of checkers."

"Speaking of unwanted company, how long is your friend staying?" Marla asked me.

I blew out a breath. "I have no idea. I've been avoiding him all day."

"Isn't it nice to have an admirer?"

I laughed. "Not when it's Rex. My parents must have told him where I went because I didn't. I should give them a call and tell them it wasn't appreciated."

"We'll scare him off eventually," Chase said.

"What's so bad about him?" Marla asked.

I buried my foot deeper in the sand. "He's not a bad guy, he just drives me crazy. If he could just be a friend or an acquaintance, I wouldn't have anything against him, but he can't get the idea of us out of his head."

Chase winked at me. "We'll convince him."

I ignored the flutter in my stomach.

"I'm going to go back," I said. "Are you all coming?"

"I am," Chase said. "Samson, come."

The dog wagged his tail and walked after us. Troy came as well, but Marla stayed behind. I had to focus on my feet, or my sandals were going to get lost in the sand.

"Hey," Chase said, suddenly looking serious. "Did you really mean what you said about selling me half of the hotel?"

"Yes."

He nodded. "Can we get started on that?"

"Sure."

"I've been looking into it. I can show you what I've found once we're back."

"Make sure you get agreements in writing," Troy said. "There are a lot of co-owners of businesses around town, and I can't tell you how messy it's been with some of them."

"How?" I asked.

"Two men owned the surf store down by the beach. One of them decided to sell out and didn't tell his partner. The person who bought it is hard to work with. It went from being the first guy's dream store to a nightmare. I get called about every other month to settle fights between them."

"I don't see us fighting bad enough to need you," I said, smiling.

"But you should have it in writing that one of you can't sell out without offering to let the other person buy you out. That way, you don't end up working with someone you hate."

"That's probably a good idea," Chase said. "But I think we'll probably get along just fine."

I nodded. "Anything else?"

Troy rubbed his chin. "There was the bead shop. It's actually right next to the surf shop. The two people who owned it became romantically involved, and then, when they broke up, they still had to see each other all the time. They had an agreement to sell to each other, but neither one of them had the money to buy the other one out."

"That would be awkward," I said.

"Those are the two that stand out in my mind the most."

Chase looked thoughtful. "Maybe we should take a week or so to come up with things to put in the contract."

"Just make sure you put in the part about only selling to each other," Troy said. "And about never becoming romantically involved. Then make sure you get it all polished and legal."

I chewed the inside of my lip. I didn't want to sign something saying we wouldn't get romantically involved, but I didn't want to come right out and say that.

"I'm not signing something like that," Chase said. "Maybe the first part, but not the second."

My heart began beating double time, and I couldn't make myself look at him to see if he was joking.

Troy laughed. "I thought you might say that."

"Well, we can't sign something like that if we're pretending to be dating," he said.

I held in a sigh. I should have known.

"But that won't be for long," Troy said. "That Rex won't stay around for long, then you can tell everyone you decided to be friends."

"I'm still not signing it," said Chase.

"Neither am I," I said.

Chase turned and smiled at me. "See, we're agreeing already."

Chocolate Chip Cookies with Browned Butter

Ingredients

1 cup (225 g) **butter**, cut into tablespoon-sized pieces
1 cup (200 g) **brown sugar**
⅔ cup (135 g) **granulated sugar**
2 large **eggs**
2 tsp **vanilla extract**
2¾ cups (340 g) **all-purpose flour**
1 tsp **baking powder**
1 tsp **baking soda**
¾ tsp **salt**

Instructions

1. Brown the Butter (The Secret Weapon)

In a saucepan, melt the butter over medium-low heat. Once melted, raise the heat slightly. Stir constantly as the butter foams and pops. You'll see golden brown bits forming on the bottom — that's the magic. As soon as it turns amber and smells nutty, remove from heat and pour into a large heatproof bowl. Let it cool until it's no longer warm to the touch.

2. Make the Cookie Dough

Stir both sugars into the cooled browned butter until combined. Add the eggs and vanilla and mix until smooth.

In a separate bowl, whisk together the flour, baking powder, baking soda, and salt. Gradually stir this into the butter mixture until fully combined. Stir in chocolate chips until evenly distributed.

3. Chill the Dough

Cover the dough and chill in the refrigerator for **at least 30 minutes** (longer if you want thicker cookies).

4. Bake

Preheat oven to 350°F (175°C). Scoop dough into 2-Tablespoon-sized balls and place at least 2" apart on baking sheet.

Bake for **10–12 minutes**, until edges are just turning golden. Centers may still look soft.

About the Author

Kristy Dixon started writing stories when she was seven and never stopped. She enjoys writing cozy mysteries and YA. At home, she spends her time playing board games with her husband and kids and writing. Occasionally she takes part in a Super Mario marathon. She has six chickens and a cat that help keep life amusing. If she isn't playing with her kids or writing, she is usually eating cookies, or wishing she was eating cookies.

Also By Kristy Dixon

Cozy Mystery
Murder With a Side of Bacon
Murder With a Hint of Cinnamon
Murder With a Fudge Brownie to Go
Murder With a Splash of Vanilla
Murder With a Drizzle of Syrup

Young Adult
The Silver Eclipse (3 books)
The Amethyst Crown
More Than Once Upon a Time

Trapped In Once Upon a Time
The Beginning of Once Upon a Time
Riviand Lost (4 books)

Coming Soon!
Murder With a Bite of Biscotti
Forgotten in Once Upon a Time
Rise of the Serpent (Riviand Lost Book 5)

Made in the USA
Monee, IL
27 August 2025

23173100R00135